MR IYER GOES TO WAR

MR IYER GOES TO WAR

Ryan Lobo

B L O O M S B U R Y
LONDON · OXFORD · NEW YORK · NEW DELHI · SYDNEY

Bloomsbury Publishing
An imprint of Bloomsbury Publishing Plc

50 Bedford Square
London
WC1B 3DP
UK

1385 Broadway
New York
NY 10018
USA

www.bloomsbury.com

BLOOMSBURY and the Diana logo are trademarks of Bloomsbury Publishing Plc

First published in Great Britain 2016

British Library Cataloguing-in-Publication Data
A catalogue record for this book is available from the British Library.

Library of Congress Cataloguing-in-Publication data has been applied for.

ISBN: HB: 978-1-4088-8165-1
TPB: 978-1-4088-8164-4
ePub: 978-1-4088-8163-7

2 4 6 8 10 9 7 5 3 1

Typeset by Manipal Digital Systems
Printed and bound in Great Britain by CPI Group (UK) Ltd, Croydon CR0 4YY

To find out more about our authors and books visit www.bloomsbury.com. Here you will
find extracts, author interviews, details of forthcoming events and the option to sign up for
our newsletters.

*To my father, whose example has shown me that
most monsters worth fighting lie within*

1

In the recesses of a brown city – almost as old as time, some say – in a home for the dying by the River Ganges lives an English-speaking Tamil Brahmin, his elder brother having sent him there to be healed of a mental affliction, or die. From the windows of his room on the first floor, through the dying branches of a Gulmohar tree, he could see the river that would, one day, wash his remains away.

If one were to examine the median of this species that is the Tamil Brahmin, they would find that this species exhibits qualities that, while having allowed them to thrive, have also helped ensure their exile from the state of Tamil Nadu. Shrewd and frugal, the Tamil Brahmin is a lover of anonymity: he works behind the scenes and never gets too close to the big man, because when the barbarians leap over the fort walls and the next batch of heads roll, there will always be a market for good accountants.

The Tamil Brahmin aspires to be the master of his private life, which he fills up with numerous comforting rituals and strictly vegetarian dietary choices, all carefully chosen for eventual transcendence. His home is a fortress of sorts, and is built following that ancient household layout where the space gets increasingly sacred as one moves further into the house, approaching the centre. He is rarely adventurous and prefers to think methodically, following prescribed routes that have stood the test of history, ritual and grandfathers; he is not one to lose himself in the forking paths of his own worried imagination.

Mr Iyer is one of those Tamil Brahmins who keeps a bamboo staff and a litre bottle of coconut oil under his bed, and listens to M.S. Subbulakshmi's rendition of 'Venkatesha Suprabhatam' every morning, much to the consternation of the formerly robust army major he shares his room with. Iyer's most precious possessions are his books and Naadi scrolls, many of them left to him by his grandfather.

South Indian *dosas* and *idlis*, curd rice, *vatha kuzhambu*, a Brahmin cook, and a Sahiwal cow kept on contract for undiluted milk consume one fourth of the monthly allowance his brother regularly sends Khanolkar, the proprietor of the home Mr Iyer occupies, even though Khanolkar's doctored food receipts claim otherwise. The rent for rooms and other amenities vary in these Kashi establishments, which were especially built to allow people to avail themselves of the honour of dying by the Ganges; most of them are run by charities and are heavily subsidised, to say the least. Khanolkar's home boasts of not just one of the nicest locations overlooking the Ganges, but also of regular visits from a doctor – educated in America, no less – TV, and cleaners and helpers who live on the premises. Iyer is Khanolkar's favourite patient even though Khanolkar really does not like him very much; his payments come in regularly and Iyer's family, who live in a village further down the river, never seem to scrutinise Khanolkar's bills as closely as some of the other patients' families do.

Iyer's complexion is weathered, and his beard flecked with grey. He suffers more from activity than sloth: most of his muscles and tendons are flexible from years of yoga, but the cartilage of his left knee has been giving him trouble. He conducts his prayers and *pranayama* faithfully, rising for his breathing exercises just before the sun peeps over the bare eastern bank, illuminating the corpses floating along the western bank of the river.

In the home, he makes friends with those who have come there to die and gain release from the eternal cycle of death and rebirth. It is in this climate of generosity, where men have nothing to lose and help sew each other's clothes, and spend their days discussing cancers or sharing inhalers, that Iyer pores over his Naadi scrolls and more recent translations of the Hindu epics with much devotion, finding hidden meanings in the lines and between them, especially when they concern transcendence.

> *Those who have conquered themselves live in peace,*
> *alike in cold and heat, pleasure and pain, praise and*
> *blame.*

Iyer spends sleepless nights trying to gauge the meaning of these phrases, which Vyasa himself, were he to come back to life, would have trouble deciphering. He reads late into the night, and again from dawn. The effort of it, coupled with the lack of sleep, make him melancholic.

I will never be young again.

He sometimes walks down to the Niranjani Akhada – that home of learned *sadhus* – where he has discussions with Himalayan hermits, graduates of much rocking back and forth and meditation in caves. But he always leaves dissatisfied. The answers he seeks come serendipitiously, from unlikely sources like Krishna, the home's doctor or the poetry-loving Bencho, whose ancestral profession of cremating the dead brings him to the home often. Upon meeting him, Iyer reads out bits of sacred texts or some English classics to him, of which *Robinson Crusoe* is Bencho's favourite. Often, Iyer goes to the ghats to look for him. Iyer finds Bencho's perspective invigorating and untainted by conventional beliefs, while Bencho is thrilled to be taken seriously by an English-speaking Brahmin who seeks his, a Dom's opinion, no less! It also does not hurt that Iyer loves a rapt audience wherever he finds it.

'It means you're supposed to forget about yourself and do what you have to do,' ventures Bencho, condensing Iyer's reflections on Lord Krishna's conversation with Arjuna while he was on his way to battle with his cousins.

Thrilled at Bencho's explanation, Iyer cries out 'you are cent per cent correct', raising his forefinger to the heavens and speeding back towards the home to reconsider the text in the light of this bracing perspective. Hurrying along the ghat, lost in his thoughts, he collides en route with a fat Marwari in the middle of his prayers. Thrown off balance, Iyer teeters before rolling down the stone steps of the bank, twisting his knee, hitting his head on a Shiva lingam and knocking himself unconscious.

The blow that has struck him on the back of his head is dull and surprisingly painless. He feels as if he has been electrocuted: his legs have gone slack and the world is gently fading from his view. When he looks back at this momentous event later, he feels that he had been transfixed, suspended in the air while the horizon rotated around him. As he loses all control, a flaming white rose blooms up in his mind. And this is how Damayanti, who lives in a house nearby, finds him – crumpled under a buzzing streetlight that the municipal authorities have forgotten to turn off this morning. Recognising him from the home, where she assists from time to time, she rushes to help him, wetting the hem of her sari and wiping his face to revive him.

The next day, a nasty bump swells up on one side of his head. The extent of the impact goes further. He stops using coconut oil, letting his hair and beard grow long and unkempt. He gives away his tape recorder, fires his cook, cancels his contract for the cow, and starts eating jalebis, naans, rotis, and even an egg on occasion. He starts having vivid nightmares where he is battling demons, sticky with blood from head to toe. He wakes from them all fevered and shaken, and writes down what he remembers in his diary. He is growing prone to losing his temper, and is becoming unbearably cantankerous. He spends long hours all by himself, and flies into rages when disturbed. Sometimes he throws things at Mattroo, the ward boy, for wearing leather sandals in his presence, certain that they've been flayed from the corpse of a dead cow. He becomes, in the words of Khanolkar, completely mad.

When the swelling subsides and he still doesn't improve, Dr Krishna prescribes Sizopin. The pills dull his senses; he sleeps a great deal. He still reads his books, but the task seems to have lost its urgency for him. Laid up with little appetite for food or life, and with his knee in a painful brace, Iyer sinks into depression.

One day, he spits out his pills on impulse after the doctor leaves the room. His dreams return that night, but this time his dream world begins to merge with the waking day.

To begin with, Iyer falls in love with his rescuer, the half-beautiful widow Damayanti. She is called half beautiful because one side of her face bears acid burns, though some say she is called half beautiful because of her dark complexion – lustrous as anthracite. To Iyer, her face represents the eternal duality of life: one side scarred, the other luminous. He searches for a name that will do her justice. A word rises up to him in a dream. He decides to call her Panchakanya after the iconic mythological heroines. To him, the name is filled with truth and significance.

Iyer hovers downstairs when she comes to the home to help one of the patients with her daily bath and prayers in the river, though he cannot muster the courage to speak to her beyond a few words of greeting. In spite of his knee, he starts going down to the ghats when he can manage, hoping to see more of her. He is filled with joy when he spots her in the holy Ganges, her sari cleaved to her skin and her scars visible only if one comes close. Iyer is keen that Damayanti remain unaware of his affections, concerned that its chaste radiance would sear them both.

One night, unable to sleep, Iyer finds his diary lying by his bed. Disturbed from reading it, he throws it out of the window.

It splashes into a puddle, drenching a low-flying crow, which veers into a tangle of electrical wires, which short-circuit and cause the transformer to explode. The bird falls, wings folding, unfixed from life. In the momentary darkness lit only by the sparks from the transformer, Iyer realises who he was in a past incarnation.

The sky has a comet.

He was Bhīma, the strongest of the Pandavas, known for his battle skills and integrity. Iyer realises that for the sake of his own salvation he has to become a warrior *brahmachari*: a transcendental soldier in search of the ultimate truth. He would need to walk the earth seeking out and engaging in adventures that *brahmacharis* got themselves into – such as battling the all-consuming demon Bakasura – and that would be the only course worth taking. Already he feels in touch with his otherworldly origins – ever-present but just beyond that which is visible – like knowledge gained in a dream and lost on waking up. He lies back in his bed, wondering when his knee will heal so he can get on with the business of immortality.

2

Underwater, Iyer grapples with the demon, his hands wrapping around the beast's slimy windpipe while its tentacles wrap around his throat like pythons, its circular jaws gnashing inches away from his face. Kicking with all his strength, Iyer bursts to the surface, intertwined with the creature that tenses, suddenly coughing into Iyer's face, knocking him into the world of the waking. He finds himself lying on his bed in the room he shares with the Major, who is coughing violently.

Accustomed to the Major threatening a violent death every morning, Iyer covers his head with his blanket, trying to sleep. But a mere blanket is no defence against the Major's experienced lungs; he coughs louder this time, with rhythmic choking at the end. Their dawns are always the same. The coughing merges with the rat-a-tat sounds of auto-rickshaws accelerating down narrow Kashi byways, political slogans blaring on loudspeakers, the bickering of vendors, the smell of jalebis frying in reused oil, the swish of mops, and the screeching of parakeets. Patients in other rooms further down the corridor add to the chorus.

At least he does not complain as much as the others, thinks Iyer. The Major is his third roommate. Unlike most of the patients here, Iyer was in good health when he joined, young for the home at just sixty. His two previous roommates had lasted less than a year each; they had been in their seventies when they'd arrived. They had cohabited with Iyer peacefully enough, but the Major and Iyer share a real camaraderie.

Easing himself off the bed, Iyer takes an inhaler off the side table and hobbles over to the Major. Not without effort, Iyer reaches for the spittoon stowed under the bed, cursing at the sharp twinge in his knee as he bends. Straightening up, Iyer helps the Major into a sitting position, allowing him to expectorate into the spittoon and wiping his mouth clean with a towel. He hands him the inhaler and watches as he fumbles with it before taking it from him, shaking it and holding it to the Major's mouth.

'Ready?'

He squirts the Ventolin into his lungs and watches as the Major's bronchioles dilate. Two puffs later, the heaving subsides, and Iyer shouts for Mattroo to assist the Major in his expedition to the toilet. He, as usual, does not appear.

Iyer helps the Major stand, lifting his bony legs off the bed – timed perfectly from his experience of doing this most mornings – and onto the floor. Together they make their way towards the toilet, supporting each other. Iyer's stiff leg makes semicircles as they proceed, and they stop every few steps for the Major to catch his breath. They finally reach the toilets at the end of the corridor, and once the Major is helped onto a European-style commode, Iyer exits the stall and leans against the sink, out of breath himself. Enthroned, and invigorated with Ventolin, the Major begins his daily expounding.

'One day the last person who would have known you will die. You will disappear from the hearts of every living being. Young people never think of these things. They do not contemplate that there will be a day when they will cease to exist completely, when even the memory of them will die. That is what we have to come to terms with, no?'

'By then, Major, you'll be dead and reborn into the body of a Chinese soldier, so it won't make a difference,' Iyer joshes, knowing full well that the Major had excelled in the Sino-Indian war even though it hadn't prevented India's sound defeat. 'You're most probably going to be reborn a godless communist, Major. You'd better hope no one remembers you!'

A wheezing laugh comes from the stall.

'How are you?' asks Iyer, walking to the stall door.

'They're taking their time.'

Iyer goes to the taps and bathes, the water chilly but refreshing. Mattroo finally lands up to assist the Major back to the room, leaving Iyer to make his way back on his own, using the wall for support. He changes into a clean shirt and dhoti and lies down, listening to the sounds of the doctor's footsteps on the stairs as he comes for his weekly visit.

The room is bare except for books stacked high against the wall, two hospital beds, two Godrej steel cupboards, a wooden table held together with brackets, an ancient Dyanora television on the wall, which goes on and off by itself, and stone floors that become slabs of ice in the winter. He had complained initially, but Khanolkar's apathy and utter shamelessness won out and eventually, the room became enough for him. From his bed Iyer can see the Major in a framed photograph on the side table, from a time when people did not feel it necessary to smile for photographs. In the photo, the Major looks outward, as though into the present, from an immense plain that stretches inwards to the distant snow-capped mountains. His platoon surrounds him, holding .303 Enfield rifles, their faces sunburnt, serious and faded. Mildew has eaten away at one edge, vaporising an entire mountain. Next to the photograph lies his Param Vir Chakra medal – legendary in the home – affixed to the photoframe by its pin.

Dr Krishna enters, switching on the tube light. The television goes off by itself. He is irritable after walking through the freezing alleys of Kashi, which, today, are cold enough to make the street dogs pile up by the tea stalls. Krishna runs an Ayurveda clinic near the Kashi Vishwanath temple. He likes his patients – people who come to Kashi to die – to whom he largely recommends the winter sunlight and not much else. He finds this more enjoyable than his previous assistant position at the S.K. Ayurvedic Clinic in Columbus, Ohio, that caters to NRIs and Wiccans, where his senior had died of heavy metal poisoning from too many Ayurvedic concoctions, leaving behind a mortgage and lawsuits that had forced Krishna's return to Kashi.

He likes the variety he finds at the home – there are doctors, businessmen, scientists and other assorted educated people, many from cantonment towns like his family, some of who have been relieved of their property by conniving children and relatives. It has made them stoic, wise and resigned. These are the sort of people with whom Krishna can discuss things that matter while their peers keep twittering on about grandchildren or the price of real estate. Krishna has made several enduring friends including Iyer, whose knowledge of the philosophical foundations of Ayurvedic practice rivals that of Krishna's teachers. Recently, though, Iyer has become a different person altogether, and Krishna's inability to find an effective cure for him greatly frustrates him.

'You hydrocephalic canned frog! Scum of the earth's core!' Iyer greets Krishna as he enters the room.

'It is going to be one of those days,' Krishna sighs. Ignoring the outburst, Krishna hands him his pills one by one. He has been considering increasing his dose, as Iyer has not been responding to the medicines like he used to. He can see from Iyer's face that he has not been sleeping. Iyer pops the pills into his mouth and drinks a little water, but slyly hides the pills behind his upper lip.

'It's time for that bedsore to be cleaned.'

'Doctor, this great soldier has been coughing a lot – too much,' Iyer says, pointing to the Major.

A voltage fluctuation makes the tube light splutter and the TV come on. A bus has plunged into the river, thirty-seven pilgrims dead at last count. A pimply reporter grasps an oversized mike with both hands and talks excitedly to camera. A slanging match between various bobbing heads on a panel follows. The anchor is apoplectic.

'Turn, Iyer,' says Krishna, taking a tube of ointment from his valise.

'The name is Bhīma.'

'Ah, yes. Yes Bhīma. Turn,' Krishna opens the tube, watching the anchor verbally assaulting a guest and waving his arms like a crab.

Iyer lies on his belly, exposing the clasps of the knee brace that Krishna removes with practised speed before applying the ointment.

'You should try to avoid the steps on the banks,' advises Krishna, unimpressed with the healing.

'Yes, SIR,' mocks Iyer.

'Are you taking your pills, man?' Krishna asks, kneading cream into the joint.

'I am,'

'Open your mouth, Iyer.' Iyer opens his mouth, the pills invisible behind his lip.

I must try another medication, Krishna thinks, getting up and closing the ointment tube, though Sizopin was the one that promised the fewest side effects. Turning to the Major, he gives him a quick once over with his stethoscope.

'What's the matter with him?' Iyer asks. 'That cough is continuous.'

'Age. Only age, Iyer,' Krishna says as he puts the stethoscope back in the valise and snaps it shut.

'You mean you don't know.'

'I mean just what I said.' Krishna swings his valise over his shoulder, relieved at the prospect of leaving the room. 'You must eat your tablets, Iyer. I know you can't see it now, but I worry what might happen if you don't.'

Iyer grins and opens his mouth, sticking his tongue out as far as it goes. 'See, nothing.'

Shaking his head, Krishna leaves and Iyer prises the tablets from behind his top lip with his tongue and spits them into his hand. Tossing aside the blanket, he hobbles to the window and, aiming carefully, drops the pills fifteen feet below into the begging bowl of Omnath, who lives under an abandoned tonga.

The Major's coughing grows more laboured as the morning progresses. Iyer tries hitting the call button several times, but no one hears it ring, as there is no electricity – not that it's answered much at the best of times. Iyer starts to get out of bed to go downstairs and summon Khanolkar from his office, bracing himself for the staircase, when the Major starts moaning. He sounds like he's struggling for breath; he stretches an arm towards Iyer, his hand pale and frozen into a claw.

'What is it, Major?'

The Major chokes and falls back onto the bed, gasping in distress.

'Someone! Please come. Hello!' shouts Iyer, calling first out of the front door, and then out the window.

'Coming!' Mattroo cries from the courtyard.

The television snaps on again. Another pimply young reporter is reporting on Jayachandra's election campaign, as Jayachandra exits a crowd, his way cleared by a small army of *lathi*-wielding policemen. A break for advertisements; the Major sits up. He is no longer struggling to breathe. He looks at Iyer as if he wants to say something, then at a point far away and collapses back into bed.

Iyer thinks that he sees his soul, like a glowing orb, escaping from his mouth, though it could also have been the vapour of his breath caught in the sunlight. When Mattroo finally appears, Iyer tells him to go and get the doctor. Krishna arrives twenty minutes later and covers the Major's face with a sheet, after a half-hearted attempt at resuscitation.

'Sorry,' he says, patting Iyer's shoulder before he leaves.

Iyer turns in his bed to face the window. The mayflower tree is bare, and Iyer hears the parakeets, the sloganeering and the rat-a-tat of auto-rickshaws accelerating down the lanes as usual. Death has been a frequent visitor and everyone knows the drill.

Soon Khanolkar would haggle over dues with whichever relative he could get on the phone. Then Mattroo would clean the room. Then Iyer would have to protect his books and scrolls from the swab water, which would slosh about the lowest *Reader's Digests*, already rotten, that prop up the real books, stacked higher for that reason.

Then fat Bencho would come by to collect the corpse, as his ancestors had done for as long as anyone could remember, which would then be taken to Manikarnika ghat, and the Major would merge with the sky and river. Mattroo arrives with Khanolkar. Haggling. Water. Swab. *Reader's Digests* soaked. The odour of phenyl. Major Rane covered up. Iyer keeps an eye out for thievery, sitting up on his bed when Mattroo swabs towards his cupboard, his arm wetting the floor in arcs, spreading the grime out evenly.

When Mattroo leaves, Iyer sits on his bed and lifts his weak leg off the mattress and onto the floor with his hands. From the lowest drawer of the bedside table he takes out the Major's revolver, wrapped in oilcloth. Unwrapping it, Iyer hefts the weapon, stands up and looks in the mirror.

An old man with a revolver. The opening frame of a comedy skit.

He is not familiar with how to use it, but the weight of the weapon is reassuring. 'Unlicensed,' the Major had told Iyer, as if its ownership made him a revolutionary. Iyer wraps the revolver up again, moves it to his own drawer and locks it, giving it a good tug to check that it's secure.

Then Iyer returns to bed, where he stays for a long time, folded like food wrapped in a banana leaf. Later that day, he hears bar-headed geese honking in the distance as they soar over Kashi, flying from Siberia. He stares at the ceiling. It stares back.

3

A few hundred yards from the home, in the shadow of a soot-covered building behind the funeral pyres at Manikarnika, a fat, drunk man in ill-fitting trousers and a formerly white shirt, inured to the odour of burning corpses and rotting flowers, tries to read from a dog-eared textbook.

He takes a breath and hopes he won't forget these lines he's practised so many times before. Before him, two perspiring, inebriated Doms – stereotyped by some for their unsteadfast habits – rest against a blackened wall after their night's duty of inflating the cost of wood while staving feet and elbows back into the flames.

Clearing his throat, he reads, the book a few inches from his squinting eyes: "'Long years ago go ... we ... made a ... try ... tryst ... tryst with desti ... nee ...'" he strains, trying to pronounce the most famous line of the most famous speech in independent India, his furry eyebrows united in concentration.

'Bencho, will you forget us when you become prime minister?' quips one of the Doms.

"'At the stroke of ... the midnight hour, when ... when ... when ...'" continues Bencho, ignoring the sniggers, but his trousers fall to mid-buttock to guffaws from the audience.

'You bastards! Once I learn English I will show you!' he hisses, pulling up his trousers. '"India will … awake to life and freedom,"' Bencho finishes in a roar, to much hooting and applause from his audience of two. Just as he is about to orate another line, he is interrupted by his cell phone, 'Yes, sir. What is it, sir? OK, sir. I will come, sir. Yes, sir. Definitely.'

Khanolkar always has a look of slight discontent about him, as if he has just found half a worm in his guava, thinks Bencho as he hurries towards the home for the dying.

When inmates at the home die, Bencho comes by and performs the necessary rituals for a nominal fee from Khanolkar, who invariably overcharges the families of the deceased. Khanolkar hates Bencho, as Bencho knows exactly how much Khanolkar is overcharging them; Bencho winks and nods at Khanolkar, sometimes mid-cremation, and it is this familiarity – more than the mockery – that makes Khanolkar seethe with rage. But still, Bencho is cheap, so he continues to be used.

When Bencho reaches the home, he smoothes his hair down, tucks in his shirt and heads for Khanolkar's office.

'Good morning, sir!' Bencho cheerfully greets Khanolkar, whose nostrils immediately flare from the tart aroma of arrack.

'Drunkard,' he snarls.

'Is Iyer Sir here, sir?'

'Sadly, yes,' says Khanolkar, closing the office door.

Mala, an old lady with dementia, pops her head out of her room, her hair in disarray.

'How is Raju? Has he passed his third year?' Bencho asks her. 'First-class distinction,' she answers, smiling.

'Where is my three hundred rupees?' Mattroo demands, standing by the stretcher, pointing a piece of bamboo at Bencho, who spins around as if he is expecting some kind of an attack.

'I gave it to your mother this morning,' sings Bencho, leaping sideways to avoid the bamboo flung at him by Mattroo. Feeling sober, Bencho runs up the stairs, dodging another missile and stopping only when he reaches Iyer's room.

Taking a deep breath, Bencho takes another shot at smoothing down his hair and tucking in his shirt. No light emanates from under the door, and the curtains are drawn. Bencho presses his ear to the door, but there is no response. Silence. He knocks lightly. There is no reply. Licking his lips, he considers knocking again.

'Who the bloody hell is it? Who the hell?' shouts Iyer from the darkness.

Reassured, Bencho enters. It is dark except for some light filtering in from the window. Bencho can make out the Major's corpse. Squinting, Bencho is able to see Iyer seated on a chair by the window, obscured in the shadow with what seems to be a steaming tumbler of tea in his hand.

'Good morning, sir. The dead body is ready?'

'What do you think?'

Bencho pulls back the sheet and closes the Major's half-opened eyes. Taking a white shroud from the backpack, he tears off a section and spreads it out on the ground by the bed. It is very thin cotton and takes time to reach the floor. They both watch it as it undulates and flutters open.

'Sir, I have request for you.'

'What is it now, imbecile? What is it now?'

'Sir, I have request for you. But first, tell me one poem?' asks Bencho, placing one arm beneath the Major's shoulder and another beneath his knees, lifting him off the bed and lowering him onto the shroud.

'Bencho …'

'Yes, sir?' Bencho says, adjusting the Major's arms by his side.

'You are useless,' Iyer says, evenly. 'I have not met a soul as useless as you.'

'Yes, sir,' grins Bencho, dropping a few rice grains from his pocket into the Major's mouth. Then, unscrewing a Bisleri bottle filled with Ganges water, he pours a few drops into the Major's mouth before quickly binding his jaw with the torn-off section of the shroud. Standing up, Bencho admires his handiwork.

'Sir, look. Rane,' says Bencho proudly, pointing at the Major, all trussed up and ready for combustion.

'Do you want a tip?'

'No, sir. Definitely not from you.'

'Well, I am not giving you any.'

'I cannot take from you, sir, except, except …' says Bencho shyly.

'OK, now you can go.'

'Except … one … poem. You are the best poet in Varanasi, sir.'

'I don't want to recite you a poem.'

'Sir, before you would recite every time.'

'Well, this is after and I don't feel like it.'

'Sir, please.'

'No.'

'OK, sir. Then I will tell,' Bencho says, removing a tin of sandalwood paste from his backpack.

'Actually, Bencho, I don't want to listen to your poetry.'

'Yes, sir,' he says, smiling, rubbing sandalwood paste on the Major's forehead. 'I am going to tell you my poem.' Unperturbed, he removes a bit of extra paste from the Major's forehead and puts it back in the tin.

'Shut up, Bencho. Take him and go.'

'But sir …'

'OK, tell me. Tell me, please,' Iyer says sarcastically.

'Definitely, sir,' grins Bencho. 'It's about my boat and also my dear donkey Trishala, sir.'

Standing astride the Major's corpse, Bencho clears his throat and recites in Hindi.

She falls off the waterfalls, drowns in whirlpools,
Dashed against the rocks, she struggles.
In search of calm water.
When will the river end?
Oh my darling, when will the river end?

'Touching. Where's the donkey?'

'Sir, it's about my donkey: she's the one who falls in the river!'

'Where's the boat?'

'My boat is worrying about my donkey, who falls in the river.'

'Ah,' says Iyer, thinking deeply for a moment, 'that does make sense.'

'Sir, mine is nothing compared to yours,' says Bencho, lifting up the Major's corpse, his arms underneath his back and knees.

'Shut up, Bencho. Shut up and get out! Poetry does not mean the same today as it did once upon a time. Once upon a time, people had self-respect. Once upon a time the learned were on top and the thugs at the bottom. The pyramid has been turned upside down. We have made sure the thugs and bandits are at the top and those with integrity at the bottom,' shouts Iyer, his voice rising with every sentence. 'Today the learned and wise have neither power nor wealth, so why would anyone want to emulate them or uphold order, law and integrity? All anyone needs to do is see where a *brahmachari* like myself – an incarnation of the Bhīma – is, to know what happens to integrity in this world.'

'Sir? Can you please pass that sheet?' asks Bencho, standing with the Major cradled in his arms.

'Don't "sir" me! The life of the *brahmachari* is the quest for the immortal in oneself. Do you understand what a quest is?' Iyer asks angrily, reaching over, grabbing the sheet and throwing it towards Bencho.

'Sir. Yes, sir. IMM-OR-tal. IMM-OR-TAL. Quest! What is this word?'

'Never mind, Bencho,' Iyer says, suddenly tired, leaning back in the chair with the tea, which has stopped steaming.

'Sir,' says Bencho, carefully placing the Major on the sheet. 'I want to ask you my request.'

Iyer does not reply; instead he leans forward and pours his tea out of the window, narrowly missing Omnath.

'Sir, I want to run for elections. I need a ticket. Come with me to see MLA Jayachandra at Kanauj. With your English and Delhi contacts, he will take me for sure. I have the whole ghat in my hand. All we need is one day. We can use my boat.'

'So you can become another thief, a looter?'

Mattroo enters with the bamboo bier and places it on the floor. Ignoring Iyer, he grabs the Major's feet and stares grimly at Bencho, who takes the other end, silent after Iyer's rebuke.

'Sir. We can take my boat,' Bencho says again, softer, lifting the Major onto the bier.

'Too dangerous, Bencho, especially with all the recent disturbances, and I am too old. Now leave me.'

'Please, sir.'

Iyer sighs and closes his eyes. They take the Major and go.

As they turn the corner, Iyer recites *Kalidasa* in Sanskrit, in his best elocution voice.

> *For Yesterday is but a Dream, And Tomorrow is only a*
> *Vision;*
> *But Today lived makes Every Yesterday a Dream of*
> *Happiness,*
> *And every Tomorrow a Vision of Hope.*
> *Look well therefore to this Day*
> *Such is the Salutation of the Dawn.*

There is a loud crash as Bencho loses his grasp of the stretcher. The Major clatters down the stairs. Mala sticks her head out of her door and issues a stream of curse-words so fast they all become one long, bilious sound.

'Beautiful!' says Bencho, his eyes filling up with tears.

'You mad fool!' screams the ward boy, rushing down the stairs.

'When did you write that?' asks Bencho, unperturbed by the Major's first steps into the afterlife.

'I didn't.'

Arguing over the division of the proceeds they were to receive from Khanolkar, Bencho and Mattroo make their way to Manikarnika ghat, negotiating their way through the crowded streets. Perched on their shoulders, the Major is light as a child.

'Bencho, this man was a soldier. He fought wars, didn't he?' asks Mattroo.

'Yes, so?'

'Don't you ever wonder what lives they led?'

'No. They're dead.'

Traffic is clogged by men stretching banners of competing parties from one end of the road to the other. They reach Manikarnika, where the river is murky and filled with children diving for the jewellery the cremated had on their persons. Boatloads of tourists float by, their cameras flashing as the Doms go about their business, stoking the pyres and haggling with relatives. Bencho unties Trishala and loads some wood on her. Then they carry the Major down the stairs, towards the pyres on the bank. They prepare the pyre, Bencho expertly throwing the larger logs atop the smaller ones. They place the Major on the pyre, feet facing south so that once released by fire, his soul can walk in the direction of the dead. After wetting the body with a little ghee, Bencho places a glowing ember on the Major's chest. Then, without ceremony, he yanks a flaming log out from another pyre and sticks it into the kindling beneath the body, allowing the pyre to burst into flame.

As the old soldier spirals starwards in a trembling column of ash, Bencho reflects on the lines that Iyer had spoken – that yesterday is a dream and tomorrow, a vision. He likes the way he had felt when he heard the lines, and he wishes that he, too, could be a poet one day. But before dreams or visions could be indulged in, he would need to collect payment from Khanolkar.

4

A peculiar feeling creeps into Iyer's life after the Major's death. He does not miss him, but his death affects Iyer in a way his previous roommates' passing had not. Iyer feels afraid. He starts taking his Sizopin again.

After the Sizopin kicks in, Iyer loses his need for answers. He lies in bed for days at a time, staring at damp patches on the ceiling, letting them be just patches and not auguries. The dampness is only dampness. His knee does not improve or deteriorate. A stiffness sets into his joints, as though they are encased in cement, and Iyer watches his junctions as if his bones belong to someone else.

Empty of argument, he finds himself enjoying simpler sensualities: the morning sun on his skin and the taste of water. He becomes acutely aware of his bowels and their timings. And from this place of meditation, Iyer begins to remember his childhood. He remembers odours and tastes – once so sharp and fresh, now dulled with time. *Time moves faster as you grow older*, he thinks.

He finds himself singing verses from *Soundarya Lahari* by Adi Shankaracharya composed two thousand years before the birth of the Jew Jesus Christ, the same verses his mother would sing during her *puja*.

> *Shiva and Shakti are one and the same.*
> *There is no place that He is not.*
> *There is no place that She is not.*
> *They are one and the same.*
> *She is the one in the three worlds.*
> *Shiva and Shakti are one and the same.*
> *That is the secret.*

With the singing comes an anxiety; Iyer thinks of his brother Arjun. On those nights, in spite of the Sizopin, Iyer is the shining warrior Bhīma: muscled and lean, fighting battles with demons.

He begins another journal.

> Bhīma looks at those he kills honestly, weighing their
> skills dispassionately. That scaly ghoul is good with
> the lance, and is cut down by a slash to his upper
> arm when his back is turned. That *rakshasa* moves
> too fast, so Bhīma knocks him down with an arrow
> to the thigh, severing his femoral artery. He stabs
> with little effort; his objective is to incapacitate as
> quickly as possible, without any confusion. Winning
> is his objective, a soldier's goal – not murder.

Sometimes when he wakes up, his hands are still holding a mighty sword that fades away as he watches.

> Arms stained to the elbow with blood, he looks at a
> large number of his cousins lying dead around him.
> The wheels of the chariots, attached to broken-
> legged horses and upturned while in full charge by
> bamboo stakes, are still spinning. The wounded

are trying to clasp their wounds shut with ever-weakening fingers, or are attempting to hide in elephant grass from the cowards searching for easy kills. The weight of a shadow on Bhīma's shoulders makes him whirl around and bury his sword into a man's abdomen, throwing him to the ground.

Iyer also writes down the details left out of the books.

Bhīma felt an indifference with victories and spent days on the long walks back home after battle, accompanying the wounded who were riding on bullock carts, groaning over the rough tracks. So much of war was bargaining with traders, camp intrigues, or the sight of orphans following the columns like scavengers. And then one had to return home and inevitably change the war experiences to suit the purposes of storytelling.

Awakened, Iyer sometimes finds that the floor of his room is covered in blood – two inches deep – immersing the *Reader's Digests*. Alarmed, Iyer invokes the goddess Durga to save him from the powers of the night. When he stops praying, the vision has passed.

Another false herald. And how many of those have I seen in my life?

Iyer starts his yoga regimen again. Lying on his back, adjusting his shoulders, pulling his navel towards his spine, breathing diaphragmatically and clenching his anus, he surrenders nightly to higher powers, begging to be delivered from his visions. Prayers done, he imagines his own funeral rites, down the smallest detail.

At the moment of Iyer's passing, the *purohit* would recite verses into his ear at close range. Iyer would listen, waiting for that glorious moment when his spirit would leave his body. All the residents of the home, led by a repentant Khanolkar, would be wailing like children, and would bathe his corpse in Ganges

water. Rice grains would be placed in his mouth and his jaw would
be bound. His big toes would be tied together. His head would
face south and the Vratodyapana rituals would be conducted by a
priest with a melodious voice, who would no doubt break down at
some point too. Bencho, with tears pouring down his face would,
in perfect English, tell the multitudes who came to pay their
respects that he owed Iyer everything. He would then recite stories
about the selflessness of his mentor. The whole city would gather
outside the home with teary eyes, aware that a great *brahmachari*
had passed. Even the Muslims would attend.

Bencho and Mattroo would place him on the bamboo
stretcher. They would hold him aloft on the walk to Manikarnika
ghat, followed by Arjun, who would be wrecked with regret at
having abandoned him, shamed by the disapproving stares of the
crowd and begging the gods for forgiveness.

Then Iyer would be set upon a sandalwood pyre, followed
by the requisite chanting and pouring of high-quality ghee. The
Dom Raja himself would place an ember on his chest. TV crews
would beam his immolation live to the country and millions
would weep uncontrollably, some shaking with grief – especially
Khanolkar, who would turn over a new leaf from that day and
offer rooms free of cost to everybody. Lying on his bed waiting
for sleep, Iyer would feel the flames licking at his neck, and when
the fire was high enough, his head would burst into blue flame,
releasing his soul from the pitiful body he had chosen for himself.

Whoosh!

It is at this point, when his head would burst into flame, that
Iyer usually finds rest. One evening, mid-meditation, just as he
is about to be released from the confines of his earthly existence,
from deep within the flames Iyer hears a woman laughing.

'Hehehehehehe.'

The door of his earthly room opens with a whoosh.

A pretty girl in tight jeans with perfect breasts enters, giggling
into her iPhone.

5

Iyer watches her as she walks in with manicured feet in gold-buckled sandals and a magenta-cased phone in painted fingers.

'Uncle?' She asks, placing a hand over the mouthpiece of the phone.

'I am not your uncle. I am Bhīma.'

Ignoring him, the woman hangs up her call and walks to the cupboard. Pushing the hangers aside, she rummages through Rane's neatly folded clothes, making a little pile of them on the floor. The white shirt he would wear on Saturdays; the singlet that Rane had darned so many times, now transparent and fragile like tissue paper. She takes out his military jacket and rests it against the pillow, looking through the pockets for money. Then his shiny military boots with metal toecaps. Turning her attention to the photograph on the side table, she picks up the medal and, together with the boots, throws it on the pile.

'Madam! That is the highest award for bravery in the nation!' Iyer says, alarmed.

'I don't need it,' she says, using her foot to push Rane's slippers out of the cupboard and onto the floor.

'Can I have it?' he asks, sitting up in distress.

'Ya, OK.' She bends over, her bottom round and pert, lifts the photo and medal from the floor and tosses the medal to Iyer, who catches it deftly.

'Who was the Major to you?' asks Iyer.

'My father,' she says, pocketing the Major's wristwatch.

'Ah. You must be Amba. He spoke about you a lot. Why didn't you come to see him?'

'I didn't have time.'

'You could have called. There is a phone here!' says Iyer, his voice rising slightly.

'Listen here, Mr … Mr?'

'Mr Bhīma,' says Iyer coldly as the door opens, letting in Krishna.

'It's not Bhīma, it's Iyer!' Krishna says, cheered at the sight of this girl with her trim figure.

'So, why didn't you come to see him?' asks Iyer again, ignoring the doctor.

She doesn't answer, tipping his drawers onto the bed and sifting through the contents instead.

'Calling doesn't take time,' presses Iyer.

'I paid for him to stay here just as someone is paying for *you* to stay here. Without me he would be in the gutter, *Iyer*.'

'Bhīma,' Iyer says, raising his voice. 'The strongest of the Pandava brothers.'

'Miss Rane here does not need to hear the story, Iyer,' Krishna says, taking his tube of ointment out of his satchel. Iyer lies on his stomach and Krishna begins to take off the knee brace.

'Silence,' Iyer says and for no reason whatsoever, begins speaking in a formal tone, much like a school teacher. 'I, as you know, am the warrior Bhīma – the winner of many battles and trysts with evil. My sworn enemy of the ages, the man-eating demon Bakasura, had been cast into the deepest pits of Narka – south of the universe, beneath the earth, in a vault made from the lowest foundations of Mount Kailash – but somehow he managed to escape from Yama's clutches. I wished to engage him in battle, but the gods warned me that battles were only for the earth and not for the heavens, where the usual parameters of existence do not apply.'

'Parameters?' asks the girl, typing a message on her phone.

'Yes, good and evil, right and wrong, space and time. Simple things like that.'

'But…'

'Please do not interrupt, and stop fiddling with your phone!' Iyer says, raising his voice slightly. Taken aback, the girl freezes mid-SMS.

'I searched for him all over the cosmos, in pestilential swamps and venomous forests, in fiery planets and in the frozen caves of forgotten moons. I transcended death to visit those shadowy realms where even the dead fear to visit lest they dissipate into the void. The beast knew I was hunting him, and since I was the only one who dared, we were connected in ways your simple human mind cannot understand. He left signs for me to follow, like poisoned rivers, noxious vapours, polythene bags and tribes with the practices of cannibalism and sophisticated rhetoric. Destiny bonded us.'

'Destiny? How were you bonded to…'

'Madam! Listen! Please!' Iyer says forcefully. 'After millennia of searching, I finally found him – more by accident than design – crouched like a ghoul over a whole civilisation that had reached an essential part of its existence: the beginning of its own annihilation.'

'Where was this?' the girls asks.

'In 1565. In a swamp near Bijapur. I attacked without ceremony, trying to cripple him as quickly as possible, but his skin was covered in scales that deflected my celestial sword. Then began the greatest battle of my life. And what a battle it was! What a battle it was.' Iyer closes his eyes tight in recollection.

Krishna and the girl smile at each other as the doctor snaps back the clasps on Iyer's brace. 'We fought continuously; his tentacles were most effective, and it was only with the greatest skill that I managed to fend them off. Some had spikes and others spat venom, while a few moved like Russell vipers with sucker ends that went for the eyeballs. We wrestled in malarial swamps within whose sludge unholy beings crawled.'

'There are no swamps near Bijapur,' said the girl, reading from her phone screen. Iyer ignores her.

'There were times it took all my will to avoid being crushed by the sheer unrelenting darkness of his being.'

'Is this really necessary, Iyer?' Krishna says, but he's ignored by both parties.

'OK. Then what happened?' the girl asks.

'Days into the battle, or maybe centuries in earth terms, we found ourselves at the edge of a terrifying abyss, with hailstones the size of Maruti cars smashing down on us. The light of a half moon illuminated the struggle. I held his jaw in what I thought was a death grip and stared into his single reptilian eye as I tried to break his vertebrae. And then something horrible happened. It was so horrible that I nearly fainted. I, the great Bhīma himself, felt terror for the first time.'

'What?' asks the girl.

'Deep in that horrible eye I saw my own reflection.'

'I can imagine your terror, really,' Krishna says, sarcastically.

'No, you cretin. My face had scales! Scales! And my two eyes were becoming one.'

'So?' says the girl.

'I was *turning* into Bakasura!' Iyer says. 'We both stopped fighting and released each other. I thought that some of his venom had infected me, but then something even more extraordinary happened. Bakasura – that infinite, all-consuming horror, the terror of ages, eater of babies – began to weep like a child.'

'Why?' asked the girl, engrossed.

'Bakasura noticed that he was turning into *me*!'

The girl lapsed into silence.

'Poor fellow, I actually felt sorry for him. Such a big fellow, crying.'

'Indeed,' Krishna adds, dryly.

'In that moment of empathy, I became more like him than I had anticipated. Seizing my advantage, I hurled him into the abyss. He fell silently, like a child betrayed. What I did not know was that the abyss led to a portal, which led straight to earth.'

'Where did he land?' the girl asks.

'In Delhi, close to the Parliament.'

'Take your tablets Mr Bhīma,' says Krishna gently, tearing the Sizopin from its foil.

'You know, I sometimes feel that I am responsible for the state of this country.'

'Wasn't Bhīma ten feet tall and very strong?' Krishna says, giving Iyer the pills.

'I had to pursue Bakasura on earth, so I decided to take the form of a human being. I appeared to one Mr Lalgudi Iyer in the middle of his meditation, and made him an offer. In exchange for his body, he could attain *moksha*.'

'And so this Iyer gave his body to you?' says Krishna. 'Just like that?'

'Yes. I became Mr Iyer, with all his memories. And life was fine for a while. But there was an accident, and he had to leave his home and come to this godforsaken place.'

'That meniscus needs time to slip back into place,' says Krishna, touching the knee brace, 'it's high time you healed.'

'Yes, doctor, sir.'

'Madam, a pleasure,' Krishna says, taking his leave. 'Would you like me to stay, or are you two going to be all right?'

'No, doctor, thank you.'

'Uncle, that was such an interesting story,' the girl says, leaning in next to Iyer, holding her iPhone high to get them both in the frame.

'No. The taking of smiling photographs encourages mental decay, self-centeredness and degenerate behaviour.'

'Two seconds. Let's express ourselves,' she says, giving the camera a pouting smile, and takes a selfie with a scowling Iyer.

'Who do you think you *really* are, Uncle? Bakasura?'

'I just spent the last ten minutes telling you, halfwit.'

'Whatever. You know...'

'We are fools. Ten thousand years ago we fought our own cousins. In 1565 we fought the Muslims. In 1857 we fought the British. In 1947 we fought ourselves. In 1984 we fought the Sikhs. In 2002 we fought the Muslims. Today we fight our own families. But *I* am Bhīma,' Iyer says, snarling, 'son of Vayu, master with the mace! Tamer of elephants! Destroyer of evil.'

She begins to laugh, partly to banish the memory of having been sucked briefly into his story. She walks backwards, unable to stop laughing.

'You're insane, Uncle,' she says, laughing. Her phone rings; the ringtone is a catchy new song. She raises her hand to answer it.

'No!' shouts Iyer, wagging his finger at her.

'What the hell, man!' says the girl, raising her voice. 'This is like, you know, harassment.'

'You accuse me of harassment? Centipede ... socialite!' stammers Iyer hoarsely, eyes wide with disbelief. As he struggles to get up on his feet, his leg brace pops open and Iyer looks down upon his knee, realising suddenly that it has not collapsed.

'I can bend my leg,' says Iyer incredulously, bending his knee; the meniscus had popped back into place.

'Who the hell cares!' the girl screams, answering the phone with one hand and throwing her father's remaining odds and ends on the floor with the other. Picking up the photograph from the bedside table, she drops it into the dustbin, the glass shattering as it hits the surface. Iyer pauses, and smiles. He is suddenly calm.

'Madam, since you are a lady, I will not precipitate you out of the window. But since you're an imbecile, I will have to avenge this insult,' says Iyer, reaching under his bed and pulling out a cricket bat. Leaping forward, the knee working perfectly, Iyer grabs the phone out of her hands.

'Be careful. It's an Apple!' she squeaks.

Iyer bellows in her face.

'AYAYAYAYAYAYAYAYAAAA!'

She screams back, 'AIEEEEEEEEEE!' her tonsils vibrating with the effort. And though his eardrums smart, Iyer notices that her perfume is lavender-based. His every sense is sharpened. Still shouting, Iyer drives the girl out of the room, squealing for help. Further down the hall, Mala screams too. The ghat dogs join in, and Iyer throws the phone high up in the air, as hard as he can, swivelling perfectly on his miraculously healed knee.

'AOOOOOOOOOOOOOOO!' howl the dogs.

'AIEEEEEEE!' screeches the girl.

'HAAAAAAAA!' goes Mala.

The phone flies out of the window and over the ghat, plopping into the dark waters. Iyer kicks open the door of his room with his newly activated leg, and tears outside.

6

First, Iyer attacks the television next door. Kapadia, whose room it is in, starts shouting at him, looking up from his wheelchair, which he tries to roll over Iyer's toes.

Bump.

'You! Leave my television alone,' he shouts, the wheel bumping Iyer's toes without rolling over them as Iyer tries to push the TV off its stand.

Bump.

'Maniac.'

Bump.

The ancient Dyanora doesn't budge an inch and Khanolkar, alerted by the racket, rushes up the stairs and into the room, waving a cane like a sword. Other denizens of the home appear at their doorways and in moments they have an audience.

'You bloody lunatic! What you are you doing?' Khanolkar shouts, ducking to avoid a vase of plastic flowers that Iyer flings at his head. They explode against the wall.

'Mongoose!' shrieks Iyer, and Khanokar bolts him into the room, forgetting about the side door. Iyer soon bursts through it into the next room, assaulting a radio in the process – this time with some success.

Two streets away, Dr Krishna has just returned to his clinic and applied leeches to Mr Goswami's psoriasis-scarred elbow in his clinic as the latter grips onto the arms of his chair, making the veins on his forearms pop. Rain clouds darken the west bank, rumbling towards the clinic. Krishna sits on the doorstep, sipping tea from an earthen tumbler and watching vehicles with loudspeakers exhort the populace to attend the election rallies.

'It's going to be a rainy night,' he thinks, just as his cell phone starts ringing.

'Iyer has gone mad! Bring sedatives! Hurry hurry hurry!' Khanolkar gasps, speaking so fast that the doctor can barely make out the words. He hears what sounds like glass breaking in the background. Before the call cuts off, he hears Khanolkar saying, 'No, Iyer, NO!'

Without delay, Krishna puts down his tea and grabs his satchel and umbrella.

'I'll be back!' he tells Goswami.

'When, sir?' Goswami asks, his eyes closed tight against the pulsating creatures drinking his blood.

'Soon. Soon.'

The doctor leaps into a funeral procession and the rainstorm breaks. Fighting his way to the front, he comes face to face with Bencho, one of the pallbearers, who is shielding himself from the sudden deluge with the stretcher, holding it straight above him.

'Doctor, where are you going in such a hurry?' Bencho asks, teeth red with *paan*.

'Iyer has gone crazy again!' Krishna says, hurrying along.

'Ah, Iyer Sir,' Bencho cheerfully moves out from under the stretcher, causing the corpse to slip off the stretcher and into a gutter.

'Wait!' shouts Bencho after the doctor as the dead man's relatives rush forward.

'You dog! How dare you? I am an inspector of police,' screams
the corpse's son, a sturdy young man swathed in white mourning,
his moustache vibrating with rage.

'Sorry, sir!' shouts Bencho, abandoning the procession and
running after Krishna.

After a few turns in the maze of lanes, they reach the home to
see a forlorn Khanolkar standing at the gate, soaked to the skin and
holding a sodden newspaper ineffectually over his head.

'It's over! I am finished.'

Krishna calmly searches through the satchel for morphine just
as Kapadia's television bursts through a window and lands on the
pavement with a loud crash, exploding into fragments. They enter
the home, led by a gibbering Khanolkar, to find the other inmates
gathered at the stairwell, baffled and fearful but deeply excited.

'It has come to kill us all! A dark spirit has risen!' Mala hisses,
whipping her head back and forth as Khanolkar, Bencho and
Krishna creep up the stairs. They see Iyer dart across the corridor,
wraith-like, and disappear into his room, slamming the door
behind him.

'We are here to help,' whimpers Khanolkar outside his door,
almost weeping now.

Krishna peers through the keyhole. Thrown against the wall,
the shadow of Iyer seems almost demonic.

'He will murder us all,' sobs Khanolkar, nudging Krishna out
of the way. Led by Bencho, they burst into the room, sending the
door and its rusty hinges flying across the floor. Iyer's traces end in
wet footprints leading towards the window. The cupboard is wide
open; clothes and books are strewn about the floor. His knee brace
lies next to the curtain. Khanolkar rushes to the window, but there
is no one to be seen on the street outside.

'He can't have gone far,' says Krishna, preparing the
morphine injection and squirting some out in the process.
Placing the plastic cap over the needle, he, too, looks out of the
window at the ghats but sees no one.

From outside the home, they would have seen Iyer on the parapet by the side of the window, his back against the wall, beard flapping in the wind. Soaked, he carries a stuffed backpack over a Mysore jacket and dhoti, his shoes tied around his neck with their laces, a scooter helmet on his head and a bamboo staff in his hand. Carefully, Iyer walks to the end of the parapet and drops the staff off the edge. Grabbing the parapet with both hands, he lowers himself slowly, his arms screaming in protest. When fully extended, his feet dangle a few inches off the compound wall. He lets go another inch, holding on to the parapet with only the first joint of his fingers when his toes find the wall. Iyer lets go and jumps off the compound wall – his feet splashing mud – right in front of the beggar Omnath, who was fast asleep under the tonga. He can hear Khanolkar shouting his name from the window above.

Rising to his feet, Iyer curls his toes, letting the mud seep out from between them. Ignoring Khanolkar, he takes a deep breath, suppressing the battle cry he wishes to bellow, and raises his face to the rain, receiving it on his face like a blessing.

7

Scurrying down the road, Iyer joins yet another one of the endless funeral processions leading to Manikarnika ghat. His chest hurts, and the exertions have given him a headache, but he has to hurry. The sun has almost disappeared into the river stretching out to his right; only its pink rim is visible.

Pulling off the helmet and ducking to reduce visibility, Iyer notices a group of lepers sitting against a step, shielded from the rain by a balcony. They are sticking their fingerless hands out – each one more disfigured than the next – looking as pitiable as possible as they beseech the crowds for alms. In front of them, a line of women stand ankle deep in the river, beating the rocks with hotel linen despite the rain pouring on them.

'*Saar, saar,*' the lepers chant, their limbs stuck out in supplication.

The end of the line is marked by a particularly disfigured leper: a surly, one-eyed man with matted hair, rotten teeth and a single working finger on each palm. A push-cart stands by his side, which he uses to transport one of his companions – a legless crone with a withered arm who sits next to the cart – her fingerless palms beating the ground in supplication.

Iyer sits next to the cart, covering himself with his blanket. The crone cannot speak, and frantically makes hand motions in his direction as he croaks *Saar* in his best beggar voice, extending a parrot fist. 'Rascal, this is our place,' the one-eyed leper threatens, wagging his single finger at Iyer. Iyer is about to inform him of his incarnation but drops his head on seeing Khanolkar and Mishra huffing and puffing down the street. They stop directly in front of Iyer, who recedes further into the blanket, clenching his fingers inwards, palm facing the sky.

'*Saaaaaar*,' begs Iyer from deep within his blanket.

'He's probably headed to the boats,' Khanolkar tells his accountant and yes-man Mishra, looking this way and that up and down the ghat.

'Yes, I'll go there. You head to the bus stop,' says Mishra, as the duo rush off in opposite directions.

'If this were Bombay I would have cut your throat by now, pig,' snarls the leper, his jaundiced eye glaring at Iyer.

'Insect, I am Bhīma: the tamer of elephants, master of the mace.'

'Go mace some elephants then, master,' the leper says, making a dismissive gesture with his finger.

Iyer looks out over the river as the rain abates, and utters a quiet prayer of gratitude for his deliverance from Khanolkar and Mishra. Sitting on the cart, Iyer feels a strange sense of comfort, even with the crone plucking at his blanket. The rain stops by the time his prayer ends. A flaming *aarti* floats past, followed by a hundred more, lit by pilgrims who have waited for the deluge to stop. Following their passage, Iyer spots Damayanti.

She is not twenty metres away, swimming in the shallow waters surrounded by marigolds and *aartis*. The sun floats low and red over the west bank; Iyer feels he has never seen such beauty. With her bathed in twilight, everything seems possible. The darkness to come holds no fear. The slouching beasts of the present recede in Iyer's imagination and his eyes fill with tears as he feels the indescribable landscape of love, his chest feeling so full that he has to place his hand over his sternum to prevent his heart from exploding.

The crone taps at Iyer's legs with her palms and says something that Iyer cannot understand.

'What is she saying?' hisses Iyer.

'She says that you are her long-lost son and that I am your father and to get lost.'

Damayanti reaches the steps leading up to the ghats and stands there, her hands joined in prayer. Then she immerses herself – once, twice,thrice – tossing her hair skywards and sending marigolds and illuminated drops of the Ganges flying towards Iyer in a perfect arc. Emerging from the water and rubbing her hair down vigorously with a towel, she walks up, clothes clinging to her body, which looks hard and lean from a lifetime of manual labour. A used shampoo sachet clings to her sari. Standing up, Iyer takes off his helmet and blanket and tidies his hair.

Damayanti spots him and smiles at 'the sad old poet' standing at the top of the steps.

'Ah, Mr Iyer, how are you?'

'Goo— gooood morning,' stammers Iyer, suppressed adoration writ large on his face.

'Damayanti, where are you, you lazy woman?' comes a call from a nearby house.

'Coming!' she shouts, turning her head back to smile at Iyer.

'Hurry up,' the voice hollers.

'What a perfect day, no?' asks Damayanti, unhurried and smiling. She spots Iyer's backpack and the helmet he holds.

'Where are you going?'

'On a journey to vanquish a great evil,' Iyer says, looking deep into Damayanti's eyes, the odour of Liril soap filling his senses.

'Damayanti, where are you?' comes the cry again.

She smiles at Iyer and turns to leave, the shampoo sachet coming into view.

'Madam.'

'Yes?'

Iyer points at her sari.

'What? Where?' asks Damayanti, arching her neck but not seeing the sachet.

As her neck stretches, Iyer can see her trapezius defined against the wet cotton of her *choli*. Her acid scars run from her cheek down to her neck, two keloids journeying beneath the fabric towards her breasts. He reaches around her and plucks away the sachet. Damayanti smiles in thanks, her teeth white against her skin. As she turns and heads off towards the origin of the shouts, she tosses her hair, which brushes against Iyer's face.

8

He's still standing there in a daze when a fat hand lands on his shoulder and yanks him into an alley. Before Iyer can exclaim, another hand covers his mouth and nose, blocking off all air.

'Bhīma Sir, it is me only!' says Bencho through gritted teeth, his breath heavy with arrack. He's surprisingly strong for a man of his size. 'See!'

Gagging from Bencho's hands, Iyer sees Khanolkar in the distance, his head ahead of his body like a mongoose, jabbing his finger at the surly leper who points enthusiastically in Iyer's direction. Iyer shoots down the alley.

'Sir! Where are we going?' Bencho exclaims, jogging after Iyer and dragging Trishala, his donkey, behind him.

'We will need a place to plan our escape from Kashi,' whispers Iyer, checking to see if they are being followed. A crow squawks, flying off a dustbin and almost colliding with his face, and then expertly flying through a tangle of electrical wires above him.

'Bencho! The crow will guide us!' Iyer says, brushing at the swarm of flies rising from the garbage.

40

'Sir? How?'

'Have no fear, my ignorant *chela*. The heavens will guide *him*.' And Iyer bolts after the crow.

'Sir? Can the heavens tell him to fly a little slower?' gasps Bencho, trying to keep up.

'We will leave in your boat, Bencho. Make sure it has supplies – enough to last until we reach my brother's home downriver.'

'I stocked the boat yesterday for a firewood trip. Isn't your older brother the same fellow who put you here?' gasps Bencho, now completely out of breath.

'We will be received as heroes and he will see our true natures. A good man, my brother is,' says Iyer, leaping over a sleeping cow.

'Sir, we can also meet the MLA Jayachandra?' Bencho gasps, lungs on fire.

'We are on a divine mission and the entire universe will conspire for us,' declares Iyer, ducking into a side street, trying hard to keep up with the crow, which periodically perches on telephone lines, as though waiting for them to catch up.

'"Within my soul I feel a rising of forgotten knowledge."'

'Within my stomach I feel hunger. I missed breakfast, sir,' says Bencho, wondering why he was exerting himself so. 'And it's my family's turn to manage the flame at Manikarnika next week.'

'Bakasura does not wait for breakfast! The sacred flame can look after itself. We have a mission. Prepare the boat!' Iyer says as he turns the corner to see the crow perched atop an enormous dreaming Vishnu. An open sewer separates Iyer from the ruins of what was once a temple complex. He leaps across it without hesitation, landing well clear of the edge, his knee elastic and supple. Bencho pauses at the drop, examining the dark green sludge ten feet below. The stench is overpowering, and something slithers in the vegetation that grows thick by the walls.

'It is too wide, sir.'

'It is not as wide as you think. Jump, Bencho,' shouts Iyer from the temple.

'What if I fall?' Bencho grumbles, releasing Trishala to graze on the lush grass around the sewer.

'It is by going down into the gutter that we find the treasures of life, now jump!'

Taking a small run up, Bencho leaps across, barely making it to the other side, grabbing onto the Vishnu sculpture just in time to prevent himself from falling. His face scrunching up with the effort, Bencho embraces the dreaming Vishnu, the god sleeping under the hood of a stone serpent, dreaming until he would have to wake up and ensure the next cycle of existence.

'Sir, what about your poetry? Can you recite some for me?' asks Bencho, distracted by the beauty of the sculpture even when its face had been sheared off by some sort of Central Asian implement five hundred years back.

'We will not recite poetry Bencho, we will live poetry,' Iyer says grandly. 'One day a sage will write about us. "Bhīma strode into the dark forest in pursuit of the demon, accompanied by his faithful warrior Bencho, riding on the noble mare Trishala."'

'Yes! You have described me perfectly. This is so true to life! And Trishala too!' Trishala raises her head from her grazing, eyes Iyer balefully and resumes grazing. Noticing Trishala chewing away, Bencho's stomach grumbles, and he is overtaken with doubt.

'But sir, I cannot leave like this. What will happen to all the corpses? Who will dispose of the dead?'

Iyer jumps off the ruins and lands close to Bencho.

'We must be willing to let go of the life we planned so as to have the life that is waiting for us. I have reached that time, Bencho, when I look back over my life and it seems to have had a plot, as though composed by a writer. Every failure and success, every mundane moment has steered me to this rock where I am now allowed to speak to you. Events that once seemed accidental or incidental turn out to have been central in the composition of this great adventure. It is eminently clear.'

'Sir, who is this writer?'

'Our lives are directed by that soul of which mere humans like you are largely unconscious, Bencho. I, on the other hand, am the dreamer of my own life,' says Iyer, stroking the axe-scarred remains of the dreaming Vishnu under his seven-headed serpent.

'Sir?'

'You are what your deep, driving desire is. As your desire is, so is your will. As your will is, so is your deed. As your deed is, so is your destiny.'

'Beautiful! How *beautiful*, sir,' exclaims Bencho, clapping energetically.

'For so long, Bencho, memories of my past lives were but flashes of strange memory: an inexplicable ache from within, a sudden familiarity, a scuttling beast at the corner of one's eye. Once, this knowledge of all lives was clear, when humans enjoyed some measure of peace and oneness with the earth, when good kings allowed their subjects the undisturbed pursuit of an inner life, before the arrival of democracy and its lumpen elements, which ensured the coming of inevitable hordes over the hills. It ended with the destruction of the Cholas and Vijayanagara, and since then clear thinking has been made very difficult. But now I know my task.'

'Sir, and it is?'

'I am looking to right ancient humiliations and regain lost honour.'

'Sir! This is fantastic. We can become famous.'

'Do not dream of the future, Bencho, think of the present moment.'

Confused, Bencho does not reply and, seizing his advantage, Iyer takes off his helmet and hands it to him.

'Let's test this helmet,' Iyer says, taking a step back, twirling his staff and breathing diaphragmatically, getting into yoga mode.

'OK, sir.' Bencho hesitates, forcing the helmet onto his head. 'But why a helmet …?'

'Because you will need it. Sit down.'

Bencho sits on a half Ganesha as Iyer twirls the staff overhead, raising it as high as he can. But before Iyer bludgeons the helmet, Bencho springs out of the way.

'Hello! Hello! Let's try it off my head!' exclaims Bencho, yanking off the helmet.

'Bencho, oh Bencho! Omnath, the great beggar sage, taught me a mantra that I recited over the helmet. Nothing can break it. Use your brains, man!'

Bencho takes the helmet off his brains and places it on a rock. Without delay, Iyer leaps into the air, bringing the staff down on it with great force. It shatters, shards flying in all directions.

'Those would have been my brains, sir – you could have killed me!' he says walking backwards, eyes wide open in shock.

'Don't be stupid. It would not have broken if your head was in it,' says Iyer, shocked at Bencho's ignorance.

'Also, what are you paying me? Nothing! Not even a token amount.'

'Did Arjuna pay Lord Krishna to ride the chariot? Did Rama pay Hanuman for rescuing Sita? Did Hanuman ask for a token amount?'

'And when I asked, you refused to introduce me to that MLA Jayachandra!' says Bencho, walking off. 'I will stay in Kashi.'

'*Chela!* Your Kashi is the culmination of defeats and sublime triumphs over thousands of years. It has been razed and looted so many times, Bencho. Down these streets horses ran, down those a mass murder, and here, a fierce battle between the Nagas and Aibak's men. Listen, I can hear the screams!' Iyer closes his eyes and inhales deeply, taking in the forgotten scene.

'So what?' Bencho says, but he is intrigued by Iyer's words.

'Dark times can call forth poetry locked within the hearts of people.'

'Sir?'

'Kashi is poetry *forced* to be a city. And we will be its poets. Do you understand?'

'Sir? All I want is that introduction, sir.'

'What is your greatest dream? Your greatest ambition, Bencho?' asks Iyer earnestly.

Bencho turns.

'My dream?'

'Yes. *Your* dream.'

'Sir, no one has ever asked me that.'

'Well then, what is it?'

'I have only one dream sir.'

'What is it?'

'I want to become a politician.'

Iyer looks at Bencho and shakes his head from side to side, utterly disgusted.

'Is that all? Do keep in mind, Bencho, that we are often kept from our goal not by obstacles, but by a clear path to a lesser goal.'

'Yes, sir. It is my goal just like Robinson Crucho; I want to have an island, but a town will do. But you cannot get fired once elected, and I can make good money. Even if you are sent to jail, your wife can stand for the elections. And my children can also become politicians and nobody can take away what we have earned.'

Iyer scoffs; as if this is child's play.

'Fact is, Bencho, I'll make you a politician in the first town I control.'

Stunned, Bencho stares into Iyer's eyes looking for signs of deceit, but Iyer is stone-faced.

'Can you really make me a politician?' Bencho asks, trying hard to control his delight.

'What do you think? Of course!'

'We need to meet that Jayachandra, and they usually ask for a lot of money. And...'

'Bencho, the word of a *brahmachari* is his bond,' interrupts Iyer, waving Bencho's questions away. 'I *said* that I *will* make you the corporator of the first town I conquer.'

'Conquer, sir? What does that mean? You will win elections?
But we will need money for the trip, and I have none.'

'Money is nothing,' says Iyer, whipping out a wad of notes
and handing it to Bencho, who takes it with both hands.

'Come with me and the world will be ours, Bencho. We will
journey into the heart of things and reclaim our country from
Bakasura.' Iyer locks eyes with Bencho. 'I promise you. Adventure
does not lie outside us, but within,' Iyer says, touching his own
breast. 'Ordinary life does not interest *us*! We want the *fantastic* life!
We will reclaim what has been *taken* from us. We shall become what
we once were – once upon a time! Because real history flows in our
veins; it not written in the books.' Saying so, Iyer leaps onto the
dreaming Vishnu, slips and nearly falls into the sewer.

Bencho rushes forward, grabbing him by the seat of his pants.

'Sir, I want *fantastic* also,' Bencho says, his eyes shining,
pulling Iyer back from the brink.

'And we will.'

'Shall we offer a *puja* before we head out?'

'No Bencho. Not necessary. Our orders come from above and
all will be revealed in our dreams. Come. *Pujas* are not always
necessary.' And with that, Iyer leaps over the abyss like an ageing
gazelle.

'Coming, my dear sir, I am coming,' says Bencho, seeing
himself surrounded with comforts, much respected, stealing only
what was meant to be stolen, and protected from all harm by his
station.

Bencho leaps across the sewer, this time landing a good foot
away from its edge, where Trishala chews steadily, unmindful of
the ways of men. Full of zeal for their coming journey, they walk
towards the river, turning their backs on the shattered temple,
destroyed hundreds of years ago by men with similar ideas of
adventure.

9

Flaming lamps light up the river and massive spotlights come on along the entire extent of the ghat. The tourist boats have been tied up, and thousands of pilgrims head to the water's edge to bathe, pray and make offerings of marigolds and floating *aartis* to the river.

Khanolkar has rented a boat, and is now plying the waters close to the banks along with Krishna, scouring the crowds for Iyer. But they miss Iyer and Bencho, who because they keep to the shadows as they move towards Manikarnika ghat, where Bencho keeps his boat.

At Manikarnika ghat, blackened buildings rise from the river enveloped in funeral smoke and the stench of burning flesh. Buffaloes wander among the pyres, and an unusually large crowd of men walk between the flames or stand atop the platforms. The Doms haggle with relatives as they stoke the pyres and turn the corpses with long bamboo staves, watched through the haze of smoke by hungry long-nosed dogs.

The boat is about a hundred metres away, six feet long and with a hull that has swelled with age and leans to one side. It has a pitted mast and a tattered black tarpaulin that doubles up as a sail, painted saffron but now more speckled than saffron.

Khanolkar gives up the search and instructs the boatman to dock the boat near Manikarnika, where Bencho comes into his view. The wind turns, blowing smoke over Krishna and Khanolkar and obscuring Iyer, who slips by unnoticed towards the boat.

'Ah, Bencho! Have you seen Iyer?' asks Krishna, covering his face with a handkerchief.

'No, sir. Iyer? Not at all.' Bencho replies, not daring to meet Khanolkar's gaze, which is seemingly piercing through his soul.

Hearing but not seeing the doctor, Iyer quickens his stride, beginning to jog. Tears come to his eyes – both from the fog and his knee; so long has it been since he has come this way. He reaches the steps leading up to the Doms' verandah, where a line of corpses are stretched out under white shrouds, awaiting their turn. As Krishna and Khanolkar's voices grow louder, Iyer crouches by the corpses beside an unlit pyre.

The boat is anchored nearby, a crow on its mast. Iyer looks with disgust at the ash-coloured water he would need to wade through to get to the boat. A large black corpse-eating catfish swims by, its dorsal fin protruding from the water, and Iyer recoils.

A few yards away Bencho is talking to an increasingly suspicious Khanolkar.

'No, sir. I have not seen Iyer. No. Of course not! How would I know where he is? I barely know him. You mean that Iyer from the home, right?'

Khanolkar does not say a word, just keeps up his stare.

'Definitely not,' blathers the unnerved Bencho, glancing in the direction of the unlit pyre where Iyer is crouching and then looking away. Following his gaze, Khanolkar leaps over the railing and rushes towards the pyre, only to find no one but a tired priest conducting a funeral, and some tired Doms, unamused by his antics.

Om asato ma sadgamaya,
tamaso ma jyotirgamaya,
mrityorma amritamgamaya
Om shanti shanti shanti

Oh Almighty! Lead us from lies,
From darkness to light,
From death to immortality,
Om, May there be Peace Peace Peace.

The priest sets the pyre alight as the corpse's male relatives view the cremation from the platform above the ghat. Nauseated by the smoke and stench but not subdued, Khanolkar tells Bencho to let them know as soon as he sees Iyer. He heads back towards the boat where awaits Krishna, still holding the syringe.

Bencho heaves a sigh of relief, but his relief soon turns to terror when the inspector whose father he'd dropped sees him from the platform.

'You! Monkey. Dog. Donkey!' the inspector shouts, jumping off the platform and landing like a cat on the banks, walking towards Bencho with his moustache bristling. Bencho walks away even more purposefully, breaking into a run and darting around another pyre that the priest has just sprinkled ghee on, preparing to set it alight. The inspector doggedly follows, pushing Doms out of his way, and corners a cowering Bencho near the pyre.

The priest scolds the inspector and lights the pyre with a flaming branch.

A red-headed American tourist materialises, moving in for a photograph.

The inspector reaches forward and grabs Bencho by his collar.

The photographer's flash goes off, blinding the inspector.

And then the unthinkable happens.

The swaddled corpse sits up, its shroud on fire, and bellows into the inspector's face, who screams and lurches backwards. Iyer rips off the burning shroud, swatting at the flames with his palms.

The redhead clicks her camera again, more out of shock than intentionally; the inspector reels backwards, and Bencho – who hasn't yet registered what has happened – shrieks like a schoolgirl. Iyer rolls off the pyre, scattering the buffaloes with his bellowing and sending Doms and flaming logs flying in all directions. Leaping to his feet, he tears off what is left of the shroud, shoves past the inspector and races towards the water, followed by a gibbering Bencho.

The inspector recovers and gives chase. From the top of the ghat, Khanolkar and Krishna watch with their mouths open as Iyer runs up the steps towards the stone balustrade, smoke still rising off him.

'Iyer! Bhīma! Stop! Your knee,' screams Krishna as Iyer leaps over a mourner.

'Come back, I just want to help,' says Khanolkar.

Iyer's knee begins to hurt, though he can still put his weight on it. He pauses on a stone platform that extends out over the river. He looks at the boat in the distance, manned by a panicking Bencho, and then towards Khanolkar and Krishna running towards him.

It would be so simple to stop this.

Pausing like an Olympic diver, Iyer extends his hands above his head in a Namaste just as Bencho pulls the stone anchor onto his boat.

No one will judge me if I go back.

'No, sir!' screams Bencho from the boat, knowing that the water is shallow. He attempts to start the boat, pulling on the starter handle.

'*Om nama Shivaya,*' Iyer intones, taking a deep breath.

I will be shown the way.

He can hear Dr Krishna's voice. 'You can't dive there! Please! No! Iyer!'

The ancient stone platform Iyer stands on is firm and reassuring.

Iyer closes his eyes and locks his stomach muscles.

His body goes slack as the twilight fades. His breathing is even. He relaxes his eyelids and through the slight gap, sees stars appear on the barren eastern bank. A sudden exhaustion envelops him. He inhales deeply, focusing on the space between breaths. His breathing slows, and a cold Himalayan wind from the river washes over the ghat.

How many people have watched the fires from this point?

Iyer leaps over the edge, crashing into the water with a belly flop. He hits the water with the sound of a very tight slap, and blacks out momentarily before sinking like a stone, the air knocked from his lungs.

The water is strangely deep, and Iyer turns to face the surface from where light shafts descend into the gloom. The water becomes clear. He hears what sounds like the calling of whales, but more melodious.

A luminous blue form floats in the depths below him. He feels no fear. Another shape moves past him and then another. Gangetic dolphins are gliding around him as he sinks. The blue form rises from the darkness, and it is a young man with the face of an angel. He swims up to Iyer and looks into his eyes, his own eyes radiating an otherworldly peace. The being takes Iyer's hand and, with a powerful kick, swims towards the twinkling surface, the dolphins spiralling around them like ghosts.

Iyer regains consciousness when his head comes into contact with the air. The murky water is about a foot deep. The riverbed is soft; when he lifts his head from the water and tries to stand, he sinks up to his ankles in the mud. He chokes and coughs out the water he has swallowed and, retrieving a staff, sticks one end of it in the mud, holding onto it like a spear. Head throbbing, Iyer sees

Bencho and launches himself into the river, swimming past the inspector, who is unable to swim, and is hence wading through the shallows.

Iyer reaches the boat, and Bencho drags him onto the deck.

'Who do you think you are?' shouts the inspector as Bencho poles away. 'You think I can't find you?'

Standing at the stern with great effort, Iyer tries to tell the inspector that he is a precocious microphallus. But he has no breath left, so he watches, his lungs slowly filling with air, as the inspector grows smaller and the blur-grey distance between them stretches.

Bencho discards the punting pole and rows towards the centre, where the river flows faster. He takes no chances, as Khanolkar might hire a boat and come after them. As they begin to float faster, he raises the tarpaulin and attaches its corner ropes to the mast and sides of the boat. It crackles open, catching the wind.

The boat reaches the centre, where the water flows fastest, and straightens up on its own. In a few minutes they are carried from the ghats and out of the city. They find themselves in twilight, wind and silence, the small clouds above illuminated on their undersides by the glow of the disappearing city.

A tremendous relief steals over Iyer and he collapses onto the deck, trying to cover himself with his blanket, oblivion engulfing him.

Home.

The tarpaulin is full of wind and crackles gently; the ropes stretched tight. The boat moves fast and straight. Reaching over, Bencho pulls the blanket over Iyer, the best poet in Varanasi.

10

When the river current slows down, Bencho gets the motor working; the engine comes to life with the rattling of its surrounding planks. Eventually, the ghostly clouds of Varanasi are left behind, and they travel between black banks, passing fields, villages and scrubland. The motor breaks down after a few kilometres, when they are going between mustard fields, barely visible in the moonlight.

There is little sound except for the dipping of the oars and a gentle wind as the travellers float under a luminous half moon, its other half crumbled into stars. Iyer sleeps without dreaming for the first time in weeks as Bencho rows steadily, his arms aching but not unpleasantly. He sweats out the arrack he had consumed earlier, the lactic acid of his exertions flowing in his arms like a clarifying agent. He imagines his political career once it has been kicked off by Iyer's introductions.

He would be fair and accept only small bribes. He would indulge in just enough thievery to keep life balanced, saving himself from the idealism his dear sir suffered from. He would get a car. A small one – no – maybe a four-wheeler, as the roads are very bad, but that would be it. No bodyguards, no foreign jaunts and no souped-up Toyota Land Cruisers like the other politicians. He would marry the most beautiful woman in all of Kashi and purchase jewellery for her once a year, maybe on Diwali, and on the New Year, of course. Given his position, he would have to pay for his niece's marriage, but he would make it a loan, interest-free, of course, or maybe he would charge a small interest for the sake of discipline.

When Bencho's arms get tired he dozes, the river carrying them along. He's woken up when the boat runs aground on a tiny island, some twenty feet across, and a flock of rain quail burst from a tree, filling the air with the sound of beating wings. He pushes the boat onto the sandbank and ties it to some reeds. They are safe now, and he feels calm. The boat tilts and Iyer – still sleeping – slides to the side. Bencho's cell phone is wet, so he takes out the battery and removes its outer case, spreading the pieces out on the deck to dry before lying down in the bottom of the boat, falling asleep almost immediately. He dreams of a white Ambassador bursting through the streets, its siren lights flashing, followed by another white Ambassador bristling with bodyguards.

The boat, jerked upright by Bencho's weight, slips free of the reeds and slides into the river, flowing upstream. It turns within an eddy and then drifts sideways.

The sound of a splash wakes Iyer. Sitting up, he realises that his face is wet. They are floating in a still lake with no banks visible, the cloudless sky one with the horizon. Iyer steps over a snoring Bencho, wiping the droplets off his face. The air is windless. The water is like glass.

The splash sounds again. Iyer turns and sees a disturbance in the water a short distance from the boat, as if something large has broken the crystal surface. A ripple heads towards the boat. As it nears, he looks down in the depths and sees a long, scaly form turn below. The disturbance rocks the vessel.

'Bencho,' he whispers, but Bencho does not stir.

Picking up his staff, he peers over the side, shading his eyes from the sun. He peers into the gloom, his cupped hands an inch above the water. As he stares, a massive crocodile bursts out of the water – jaws agape – grabs him about the head and shoulders with yellow teeth and yanks him into the river.

11

Shock. Water. Teeth.

Iyer's arms are pinned to his sides as the crocodile attempts to swallow him whole, shaking him from side to side underwater, a muscular peristalsis urging him down its undulating gullet, which presses relentlessly around Iyer's face.

God save me.

Iyer wakes with a yell – this time for real – waking up Bencho and startling a rhesus macaque that has leapt onto the boat from an overhanging branch.

Sitting upright with shock, Iyer shoos away the monkey, which bares its teeth and walks away across the bow, upright. It puts a hand on its hip, unlike any monkey Iyer has seen before. Still startled by his dream, Iyer notices the foam. It fills the surface of the river in thick clumps, sometimes ten feet high, and bubbles blow about them like confetti. The monkey attempts to jump onto a branch attached to a dead tree and fails, landing in the foam and into the invisible river with a muted splash. The froth moves as it swims to the bank unseen. The monkey pulls itself out of the water again, flopping down in the mud like a drunkard and turning glassy eyes towards Iyer.

Iyer is rattled.

'Bencho?' he says, panicked. 'How long have we slept? Where are we? What was that?'

Bencho rubs his eyes and takes in the landscape, a chemical smell filling his nostrils. The water is invisible, the banks are lined with dead trees, and it looks as if the boat is floating on frothy milk. Little rainbows appear and disappear in the mist. Iyer shakes his head, willing the vision to pass, but it is no vision. He leans over the side of the boat and waves away the bubbles to reveal the black water beneath. Taking a handful of it, he smells it and wrinkles his nose in disgust. It's cold; he buttons up his Mysore jacket.

'We are approaching a dark place, Bencho,' Iyer says cryptically, his knee beginning to ache with the previous day's exertions.

'Yes, sir, I think this is the opium factory in Ghazipur. And now there are many other factories here too.'

'No, Bencho, that monkey was a messenger sent to warn us.'

'Sir, that monkey was high on opium. They eat it from the factory.' Bencho says, checking his cell-phone parts, which seem to have dried.

'Quiet! You are unaware of the dangers here.' Iyer says, using his staff to push the boat away from the dead shores while scanning the foam for crocodiles.

Bencho snaps the rear cover onto the phone and switches it on. He holds it in front of Iyer's face. A wallpaper shot of Mount Kailash, the abode of Lord Shiva, appears before the phone goes dead.

'It is not working,' whimpers Bencho.

'We have bigger things to worry about, Bencho. We are not in our world.'

Iyer takes over the punting pole and grunts as he punts them through the alien planet.

'It's my phone! Also we cannot tell the time as neither of us have watches.'

'Bencho, we live in the centre of time. We are bordered by the dimming glow of the past and looked down upon by a fathomless future. We live in the briefest of illuminations, the slightest glow, the barest flicker. An eye blink! Time cannot be told, so do not fear, Bencho. It is only mere mortals of the ape variety who use cell phones to tell the time. The *brahmacharis* of ancient times never had cell phones.'

'I saved up for this,' Bencho says, wringing his hands.

'*Chela*, we should be able to tell the time by the passage of the sun and the lengths of shadows, both from the sun and the moon. We have lost touch with all this. It is time to rediscover it.'

'Sir, I am worried.'

'Can I help you to get rid of your worry?' asks Iyer in his sweetest voice.

'Yes, sir, please,' requests Bencho, handing the phone to Iyer, who promptly hurls it into the foam.

Bencho turns to Iyer and stares, too stunned to speak for a moment.

'Why did you do that? That's the only phone we have!'

'No phone, no time, no worry,' replies Iyer, flopping down on the deck and stretching out his legs as if he is relaxing on a picnic.

We journey into the heart of things.

Not placated by his philosophical approach, Bencho rises to his feet. Sensing battle, Iyer grabs his staff and leaps to the bow, whirling around in a crouch, eyes narrowed.

'Bencho, I have been trained by the gods to defeat anyone.' He twirls the staff.

'Sir, I paid extra for the internet plan,' hisses Bencho, cracking his knuckles.

Iyer makes a move, feinting with the staff. Bencho nimbly avoids the stab, grabbing Iyer in a headlock as Iyer grabs Bencho's thigh, lifting Bencho's foot off the deck. Grunting and gasping, with Bencho on one leg and Iyer's head under Bencho's arm, Iyer's face turns blue – neither able to get the better of the other.

A sound reaches them over the water: a human scream merged with another sound, the screeching of metal on metal, knife on a lathe.

'Bakasura!' says Iyer, extricating himself from Bencho, who freezes.

'No, sir, machinery.'

'He is near, Bencho.'

They hear the scream again, and it is unmistakably human.

'Let's leave,' says Bencho, grabbing the punting pole, the scuffle forgotten.

'Coward!'

Iyer leaps into the shallow river and pushes through the water, moving through the mist towards the sound. It comes from the left, or maybe the right.

He pauses, listening hard, and changes direction.

Another scream, and he turns again as Bencho drags the boat up onto the bank, begging Iyer to stop.

'Sir, the cops will harass us if we're witnesses. *Please* let's go!'

Ignoring him, Iyer runs into the mist through the dry reeds that crumble into dust when he brushes against them. He emerges in a dry lake bed filled with the boles of dead trees, their roots covered in motor oil and plastic litter. A dead place.

A lone, emaciated *sadhu* sits cross-legged in front of a gigantic rotting stump of what was once a banyan tree. Above him, a tattered banner reads that he is on hunger strike to save the Ganges from industrial pollution. Iyer folds his hands together as they pass him and climb the embankment surrounding the lake bed.

Iyer sees the top of the opium factory as he walks on the crest of the embankment; the troughs show him roofs filled with black opium, stretching all the way up to a stained building surrounded by barbed wire. A fabric mill belches smog from massive stacks some distance away. Ahead, to the left of the banks, small tanneries eject effluent into the water. The smog merges with the mist and flows over the embankment and into a shanty town, which opens onto the river, its bank crowded with trucks. Skinny figures dot the landscape, bent under loads, shouting to be heard above the sounds of an unoiled earth-mover that mines black sand from the riverbed and onto a truck.

He stumbles down the embankment, slipping, knee-deep in sludge, and swatting away flies rising into his nose and eyes. Out of breath, he finds himself in the midst of trucks and loaders as he runs along the open drains of the runoff, whose concrete edges are used as latrines by the residents of the shanty surrounding the factories. He walks down an alleyway, past listless men crouched in the shadows, drinking tea from disposable plastic cups that litter the streets in hundreds, past a bent old woman with face tattoos carrying a pot of water over piles of rubble. A child urinates in the middle of the street. Langur monkeys lie on parapets, stoned and slothful but still watchful.

'Where are you?' Iyer shouts, scrambling up a mound of coal.

'Sir, I am here,' cries Bencho, at a distance.

'Not you! The one who screams!' shouts Iyer, standing on top of the crest and searching the grounds ahead, his view obscured by the branches of a rain tree.

'No more, please,' someone cries. It sounds like a child, and it seems to come from near a truck close to the river.

'Aha!' shouts Iyer in triumph, but the coal ridge he is standing on crumbles under his feet, sending him tumbling down its side, picking up speed as he goes. He tries to stop his fall, losing his staff in the process, as he skids head first into an open pit at the base of the pile. As the dust clears, Iyer comes to: arms pinned to his sides, immobile in absolute darkness, upside down in a manhole with his face inches away from a flowing stream of sewage and chemicals.

A clicking sound surrounds him: the sounds of tiny wings snapping and little feet scuttling. Iyer senses feelers probing his lips and nose. A tiny beast runs over his eyelids. Dazed, Iyer tries to shout, which he does with his mouth closed and teeth gritted.

'Bencho. *Bencho*!'

The sound echoes in the pit that extends into a larger network of sewers beneath Iyer. His eyes grow accustomed to the darkness as the surface below his head undulates.

Bencho rushes about the piles, finally spotting Iyer's staff at the base of the coal pile. Peering into the manhole, he sees Iyer's wiggling feet about two feet below.

'Sir!'

'Get me out of here!'

Wrapping his scarf around his face, Bencho reaches into the open manhole, but Iyer is too deeply lodged for him to reach. Hooking his foot around a root that snakes out of the coal pile, he lowers himself into the hole and grabs Iyer's feet with both hands.

'This is Bakasura's doing!' Iyer concludes as Bencho attempts to lift him out, groaning with the effort.

'No, sir, these covers have been stolen,' gasps Bencho, 'It is eight hundred rupees for one manhole cover, sir.' Bencho heaves away, gagging from the stench, his face red with exertion.

Bencho puts all his strength into a terrific yank that dislodges Iyer, sending light streaming into the space beneath him. Blinking in the sudden light while still upside down, Iyer shrieks. The ground beneath his suspended head undulates with a sea of cockroaches. Several fly up to his head, and one scuttles across his eyes. More scurry up his sides and onto his body, reaching Bencho's hands.

Still shrieking, Iyer is hauled up the hole. Like a volcano erupting, the roaches follow, running up his body onto Bencho's arms, who begins to shriek as well, trying to whack them off with one hand and almost losing his grip, sending Iyer falling a few inches back into the pit.

'Do not let go! Do not let go,' begs Iyer, and a roach takes this chance to run into his open mouth, making him gag and spit.

'Sir, I cannot hold you,' moans Bencho, wide-eyed with disgust as a cockroach alights on his nose, its feelers tickling his forehead.

'No, Bencho, please! Have courage!'

Bencho heaves on Iyer with all his strength once more. Like a cork from a bottle, Iyer bursts out of the manhole and lands on top of Bencho. Rolling on the ground, they slap at their bodies, frantically plucking roaches out from inside their clothes. When Bencho thinks he is done, a tickling makes him look into his briefs; when he checks, a shiny, clicking specimen flies out of his underpants.

'Let us leave this place, let us leave this place *for ever*,' Bencho sobs as they stumble away from the pit, collapsing within the roots of a rain tree.

'That was no manhole,' Iyer maintains, gasping and breathless. 'I had fallen into a trap dug by Bakasura, a coward, no less.'

'No, sir, my cousin Babli steals these covers.'

The exchange is interrupted by a piteous scream.

'It is only an earthmower, sir; they make this sound when they haven't been oiled. Let's go, sir.'

Ignoring his breathlessness and the bruises on his elbows, Iyer picks up his staff mid-stride and runs towards the scream.

12

Bencho follows as Iyer races along the bank, deserted except for the odd truck being washed. They come to a truck marked Jayachandra Transports. A tall, thin man with greasy hair beneath a white skullcap is chasing a skinny teenager in grease-stained clothes around the vehicle, trying to hit at him with the buckle end of a belt. Neither of them see Iyer till he shouts out to them.

'Mongoose! I am Bhīma, protector of the innocent. Unhand that child or die.'

The boy pauses, and the driver catches him, forcing him into a crouch and raising his belt.

'Stop!' Iyer commands.

'This dog stole from me,' the tall man says, looking a little undecided about his next course of action, given that two strangers – both filthy, with one wearing a suit jacket, and sounding educated and thus dangerous – have approached him from the bushes.

Bencho, seeing an opportunity, rushes forth, looking to the left, as though someone is present in the bushes, 'Inspector Sharma, cover the right; Inspector Ghosh, go to the left! Tell the constables to check near the river.'

The tall man stares long and hard at Iyer. Something about him doesn't add up. A cockroach runs out of his trouser leg and scuttles away sideways.

'What is your good name and what the hell are you doing?' asks Iyer in English.

'Sir, I am Aurangzeb, and I am a truck driver. My errand boy stole petrol from the truck.'

'Aurangzeb?' barks Iyer, confusion flickering across his face. 'You again! You inflictor of humiliation and renderer of shame! I command you to release this child!' And Iyer swings his staff at Aurangzeb, whacking him on the side of his head. Iyer's opponent crumples to the floor, from where he feebly raises an arm.

'Sir? I am only a driver. What will I tell my employers about that missing diesel? I will have to pay for it from my own pocket,' he says, touching his head where the wood made contact and finding it sticky with blood.

'Is that so?' Iyer asks. Perhaps this unkempt truck driver wasn't that Mughal villain after all.

'Tell me child, is this true?' Iyer asks, his eyes boring into the lackey's.

'Of course not!' the boy says, 'I only took ten litres, and that too because he hasn't paid me. Also, sir, he keeps a portion of my salary for himself, as commission, he says.' The boy scratches his clavicle, which seems to pop from his shoulders.

'How much does he owe you?'

'Five hundred rupees, sir.'

'You stole more than ten litres! That's more than five hundred,' shouts the truck driver, pressing on his head wound with a handkerchief.

Iyer rushes forward and raises his staff over Aurangzeb, who raises his other hand to protect himself.

'Aurangzeb, what you put out always comes back at you, my friend, in one life or the other. Pay him or I will beat you to death!'

'Sir, he is like my little brother. I swear I will pay him,' whines Aurangzeb, 'but later. My money is at home. By by my life I swear it,' he says, lowering his raised hand and placing it over his breast.

'Do you swear that you will not loot this child, and pay him what you have stolen from him?' Iyer asks, his staff still raised over the Aurangzeb's head.

Bencho yells into the bushes, 'Constable! Seize this vehicle.'

'I swear on my mother, sir,' beseeches Aurangzeb, plucking at the skin of his throat and looking Iyer full in the eye, holding his gaze until Iyer lowers the staff.

'See, sir,' says the truck driver, and takes his wallet out, removing several notes and handing them to the boy. 'I will give him the rest later.'

Somewhat satisfied, Iyer lowers the staff. 'Child, when you go to Kashi next, tell the famous Panchakanya about my bravery here.' And without another word he wades into the water, taking a shortcut to the boat that is tied to a branch at the bend. Confused, the errand boy looks at Aurangzeb, whose eyes narrow as he looks at him. Iyer is in waist-deep when the boy shouts after him, wading into the river.

'Sir!'

'Yes, child?'

'Can I come? I will get off at the next village.'

'He has given his word!' Iyer says, reaching over to cup the boy's face in his hand. 'Have faith, my child.'

The child bites his lip, realising beyond any doubt that his rescuer is indeed insane. Getting onto the boat, Iyer is overcome with emotion. He feels with all his heart that he is on the right path. Bencho starts the motor and they leave the duo behind, the boat nearing the next bend in the river.

Iyer begins to sing a verse from the *Gita*.

> *Your right is to the duty only, not to the fruits thereof.*
> *Do not act for the results of your deeds.*
> *Never be attached to not doing duty.*

Overcome with joy, Iyer hums between verses as Bencho mans the engine. The river's course has changed due to sand mining, so Bencho negotiates the gouged sandbanks, steering the boat towards the darker, deeper waters.

'Sir, that boy was a rogue. He betrayed his boss. He stole from that driver. He had a shifty look about him,' says Bencho as Iyer hums, examining a splinter wound on the webbing between his finger and thumb.

'It is not the business of the *brahmachari* to discover whether the beaten are reduced to their circumstances by their vices or virtues, Bencho. I only have eyes for their suffering, not their misdeeds.'

'But sir ...'

'When there is no justice, one invokes the gods. I answered that child's prayer and nullified any previous misdeeds that I might have inflicted on him in some other incarnation. Today we are one, that poor child and I. That boy's destiny and mine are *intertwined*, Bencho.'

Iyer starts singing again, louder than before.

Never be attached to not doing duty.

'What about Aurangzeb's destiny? Is his destiny also *intertwined*?'

Iyer ignores him, singing as he picks at the splinter in his hand.

As the boat turns the bend, the truck driver snatches the notes from the boy and grabs his throat. Picking up his belt, he hits the boy across the face so hard that a shaky tooth flies out onto the sand. Then he kicks the boy on the buttocks, sending him into the side of the truck. The pleading and screaming resume, accompanied by the unoiled earthmovers gouging out the riverbed.

Bencho hears the screams and rows faster, while Iyer, overcome with bliss, is lost in song.

13

The foam dissipates as the river curves away from the factories on the bank. They begin to come across treeless hills growing vegetation, and little fish with shoals rippling the surface reappear. Iyer and Bencho wash with buckets of river water, and dry off in the sun. A kerosene stove, a dish, and a gunny bag half-filled with food supplies appear from beneath the floorboards, and Bencho cooks rice and *bhindi* under the tattered awning, shielding the flame with his body. He serves Iyer in the only steel plate they have. Iyer takes the plate to the bow, at a safe distance from Bencho, and eats with his back to him. Bencho waits for him to complete his meal before beginning on his own.

When he is done, he gives the plate to Bencho, who washes it in the river. Then he puts away the plate and eats from the dish, wolfing down the food. Bencho is licking his fingers when another familiar odour makes him rise in alarm. Motioning for silence, he punts the boat towards the bank, taking care not to splash. A small village comes into view, burnt to the ground.

'He is here,' Iyer says, reaching for his staff and poking it at the lily pads. A bullfrog breaks the surface behind the boat and vanishes, popping up again a few feet away. Iyer strikes at it with his staff. It disappears again and then rematerialises further in the water.

'Bakasura!'

Bencho sees three bodies floating on a pool beneath a banyan tree, its roots descending into the water like curtains. They are male, and floating face down in the maroon water. Still communing with the frogs, Iyer doesn't notice them, and Bencho punts the boat away from the banks just as a light patter of rain starts falling. As he rows away, the rain starts in earnest.

Ahead of them, the river breaks into two. The right stream is overgrown and fast flowing. The left is wider and leads into a large lake that exits into another tributary. A flock of black ibis takes off from the bulrushes and flies low over the boat, swerving to the right.

'We should take the left,' shouts Bencho as the heavens open up further, water falling in ragged sheets, stinging their bodies.

'But the birds fly right!' Iyer counters, standing at the bow, his clothes whipping in the wind, trying to cover himself with a piece of tarpaulin.

'That could lead to rough waters, sir,' shouts Bencho, barely audible over the hammering rain.

'No matter. We can stop and carry the boat overland if we need to. We must follow them.' The wind is so strong the boat leans to one side, forcing Bencho to realign himself to right it.

'Sir! No! The boat is too heavy and the left is easier. I swear it.'

'No, Bencho! Right!' shouts Iyer.

'Left, sir!'

'Right, Bencho.'

'Left, sir.'

The river decides for them as they near the junction and a powerful current spins the boat in a half circle, nearly knocking Iyer off his feet. Bencho loses his footing, only barely holding on to the mast as the boat plunges into the rapids on the right tributary, hurtling into a cataract of foam and rocks. Lurching to the bow with great effort, Bencho uses the punting pole to steer the boat away from the slick, jagged boulders, as Iyer holds on to the mast of the hurtling boat. It is several minutes of pure terror before the river slows, widening into a plain.

The rain reduces to a steady downpour. Grateful for their safe passage, they travel for some hours, finishing the cooked food, which Bencho scrapes from the dish with a teaspoon.

'We shall rest the night at a town,' Bencho says, poling the boat with renewed vigour at the thought of hot food and a dry bed as Iyer sits at the bow, wrapped in a tarpaulin that chatters in the rain.

The boat passes under an old crumbling stone bridge some thirty feet high, a hole where the brass plaque naming its builder was once held. A flock of fruit bats hang underneath it, protected from the rain, clicking away.

Hearing a woman's screams, Iyer's head springs from within the tarpaulin; Bencho rolls his eyes.

'Sir, just because people scream doesn't mean ...' begins Bencho, already dreading where this might go.

Accompanying the scream is the sound of music.

'*Chillaaoo, aur chillaaoo ... yahan se tumhari awaaz kiseeko bhi sunayi nahin degi ... ab tumhe bhagwan bhi bachaa nahin sakta.*'

'A scream, Bencho!'

'It's a movie, sir.'

'No, Bencho, a scream is a scream, no matter where it comes from.'

'No, sir, it's a scream *from* a movie. That's why there is music playing.'

'Bencho, I hear a celestial choir,' Iyer says, his face relaxing, reaching for his staff. 'They call me to action.'

'Sir, there is no celestial choir.' Bencho pulls at the engine's choke.

'Only a true *brahmachari* can hear music like that,' Iyer says, throwing off the tarpaulin and leaping to his feet.

On the bridge, a man in a soaking-wet black safari suit and an eyepatch pushes a white Ambassador car, its roof marked with a red government beacon. Another safari-suited man in a turban holds the wheel. A handsome woman sits in the back, looking at a small TV on which a villain is about to fling himself on a supine female form.

'*BACHAOOO!*' the heroine screams as the villain leers.

'She cries for help!' shouts Iyer, trying to make it out through the rain.

'Sir, please! She's watching a movie.'

Ignoring Bencho, Iyer leaps into the shallows and scrambles up the embankment.

'I swear to God, sir, you're charging a TV!'

Iyer is already on all fours, climbing upwards towards the road. He catches up to the car and walks past the safari-suited man pushing it.

Iyer knocks on the rear window.

'Madam? Madam?'

The woman unrolls the curtained window a few inches.

'Yes?' she asks. Even though it is raining and the interior of the car is dark, Iyer can see that she is light-skinned with full lips and large almond eyes that flash back at him.

'Your highness, I am Bhīma of Benares, a *brahmachari*!'

Her eyes widen, intrigued.

'I am on a quest to defeat Bakasura, and I could not help but notice your predicament in these dark times. Are these men trying to kidnap you?'

The woman looks at Iyer's well-worn and soaked Mysore jacket and then into his eyes, unblinking and kind, unable to figure out what's going on here but gauging that it is truly fascinating.

'Yes, of course they are,' she says, a suppressed smile at the corners of her mouth.

Iyer nods in a gesture of reassurance. He withdraws from the window and allows the car to roll past him. Raising the staff like a cricketer, Iyer swings it with all its strength and brings it down across the buttocks of the man pushing the car, connecting with a sound much like a gunshot. The man stands to attention, open-mouthed in shock, grabbing at his rear as Iyer whacks him again, hitting him across the fingers the second time. He yelps in pain, grasping at his fingers.

Calmly walking behind the stricken man, Iyer grabs him by the scruff of his collar and the seat of his pants. He pushes him off the embankment, where he tumbles past Bencho, himself in the process of crawling up towards the car. Reconsidering, Bencho slides back down the slope and jumps back into the boat.

Above Bencho, the driver has braked and sprung out of the car, armed with a jack rod. He wears tailored polyester trousers and shirt and has a beard that descends to his waist. Well over six feet tall, he towers over Iyer.

Iyer lunges forward without hesitation, knocks the jack rod out of the man's fingers and, as he wrings his hands, Iyer pivots on the staff, swinging full circle and hitting the giant on the side of his head, sending him sprawling onto his back.

The woman watches from the slit in the window as Iyer throws himself at the driver, knocking him to the ground. Enraged, the driver sits up and sends Iyer sprawling with a swing of one massive arm. Standing up, he lifts Iyer up as if he were a doll, crushing him in a bear hug. Kicking backwards, Iyer scrapes the man's shin and hits him with the back of his head, getting him full on the nose. The giant drops Iyer, who picks up his staff and twirls it, preparing to send the driver into his next incarnation.

'Spare this man, Mr Bhīma. He is not deserving of such a death.' The voice belongs to the beauty who has alighted from the car. She is wearing a bright red sari draped over a low-cut *choli*, all of it made yet more enticing by the rain, which appears to be tapering off.

'Madam, allow me kill this polyester-panted pervert. He deserves no other fate.'

'Pervert?' splutters the giant. 'Lunatic! You dare call me a pervert?'

Shushing the driver, she turns to Iyer, 'Please sir, spare him. He is just a misguided fool.' Her eyes are pools of innocence.

'I shall obey you, dear queen,' Iyer says, lowering his staff.

'I'll spare you on one condition, you degenerate. Go to beautiful Panchakanya of Benares, fall on your knees and tell her about what I have done today in her honour.'

The driver quivers with rage, but seeing the lady winking at him over Iyer's head, he manages to prevent his fist from smashing Iyer's face. Disgusted but resigned, he turns towards the car, which Iyer sees as an opportunity to prod his buttocks with his staff.

'Dara, no,' says the lady.

Livid but still controlling himself, the giant exhales and keeps walking.

'Go and do Mr Bhīma's bidding, Dara. Where did you say she was?'

'My *chela* Bencho will show this imbecile the way. Bencho?' says Iyer.

'GO NOW!' the woman says, knowing full well that in a few seconds her presence will not be able to save Iyer.

'Sir,' comes a distant yell.

The bushes at the side of the road part, and the man Iyer had shoved down the embankment emerges, murder on his mind.

'Go and meet the boatman with Dara,' she tells him as he approaches Iyer. The man reluctantly obeys.

'It's not a good thing to kill my only bodyguard, Lord Bhīma!' she tells Iyer, her eyes twinkling.

'You said you were a prisoner, madam?' Iyer asks, surprised.

'Yes darling, a prisoner of boredom. And my name is Ranjana. Queen Ranjana, if you like.'

'Boredom? I have risked my life to defend you, my queen,' Iyer gasps, shocked at the pretence. 'And is that leather?' he asks, noticing the upholstery and peering into the car, horrified. 'Cow skin!'

'And you freed me of my boredom, you funny man! Are you doing all this for love, for your Panchakanya?' Ranjana grins, leaning against the car and playing with a large diamond on her ring finger.

'Yes, queen. For love and more.'

'Lucky lady,' Ranjana says with twinkling eyes.

'She is not lucky. She is who she is. Timeless,' Iyer says. 'Only I can see her true beauty,' he adds.

'What about my face? Can you not see its true beauty?'

'Yes, my queen, I can see your face,' he says, stammering.

'And? What do you see?' she asks, standing up straighter and coming closer to Iyer, leaning forward just a bit.

'My queen?'

'Am I not beautiful, dear Lord Bhīma?' Ranjana asks, moving closer still.

'You are indeed attractive, my dear queen, but ...' Iyer starts to back away, his voice trailing away.

'But what? Why are you moving away? Can you not offer a few words of timeless wisdom to a lonely queen?'

'My queen, do not forget that I am a *brahmachari*, sworn to the pursuit of ultimate truth,' Iyer finds himself stammering, his throat locking up as he backs into the car.

'Lord Bhīma, do not forget that I am just a simple girl with simple needs,' Ranjana says, grinning.

'Pleasures conceived in this world have a beginning and an end, my queen. They lead to misery if left unchecked.' Iyer straightens up and attempts to regain his composure. 'I do not know my own powers, my queen. You might be turned to ash if you are not careful,' he says, heart racing.

'I can certainly feel the heat. It's so hot,' Ranjana says. 'Come, let us retire to the car and drink some cold coconut water, and relax and be happy.'

'Bencho? Where are you?' Iyer shouts, but gets no reply. 'A man must overcome his passions to find truth,' he says hoarsely, his back against the open door of the car.

'Well, Bhīmaji, does it look like I am a man?' Ranjana says, leaning further into Iyer, who stumbles backwards into the car and onto the leather.

'*Om nama Shivaya*!' he yells and flees the car, sliding down the embankment and into the river. Tripping in the shallows, he stumbles onto the boat, Bencho and the giant looking at him strangely.

'You will never tempt me! I am sworn to Panchakanya of Benares. Bencho!' Iyer shouts, pulling the boat free from the reeds. Bencho leaps into the boat and begins to row it with gusto.

'Sir, what happened?' Bencho asks in between grunts.

'Shut up Bencho. Keep rowing! And until we triumph in our endeavours, we shall not stop.'

'Stop what?'

'Bakasura, you fool.'

'I am not a fool.'

'Yes you are.'

'I am not a fool.'

'Imbecile. Baboon.'

'Sir, what is an imbecile?'

Watching the duo, Ranjana giggles, delighted at Iyer. It is not every day that one meets a real character in the cow belt, especially a lunatic who speaks perfect English. Even the giant shakes his head from side to side, a little ashamed of his previous rage. It is not his way to rough up the mentally unhinged.

'Find out where that fool lives.'

'Madam?' asks the bodyguard, confused. 'Why?'

Her hand darts out and slaps him across the face, her diamond leaving a gash on his cheek.

'Just find out!'

14

A dark cloud hovers over Khanolkar at the home. Iyer's brother had been informed of his escape, and in spite of Khanolkar telling him at length and as politely as possible about the property damage, there was to to be no cheque forthcoming to cover it. He had, at least, not been as furious as Khanolkar had feared on hearing that Iyer was at large.

News of Iyer's exploits has filtered back to Kashi. The local constable said he had heard that Iyer had become a *dacoit* himself, joining one of the Chambal gangs, and the sweeper had heard that he had saved a woman's honour. A tea vendor told Khanolkar that Iyer was suspected of being behind a violent caste-war raid on a village. The barber had heard that Iyer had joined a travelling group of bandits, and the local ear cleaner said he'd heard that Iyer had thrown a man down a mountainside so savagely that he'd fractured his pelvis, causing Khanolkar to feel a sharp pain deep within his own pyriformis. His migraines had returned, taking him to Krishna's clinic for a head massage.

Sitting on a chair by the door, his knobbly shoulders covered with a towel and surrounded by jars of fat tiger leeches, jars of

Ayurvedic herbs and concoctions of varying hues and colours, Khanolkar lets Krishna pour warm coconut oil on his scalp. The doctor kneads his bald pate, pinching the skin behind his head and stretching it periodically, releasing it and repeating the process.

'That fool will destroy my name,' Khanolkar says, eyes half-closed as Krishna raps his forehead with two fingers. 'He's a madman on the loose. What if he murders someone? They will *definitely* come for *me;* God knows his brother's not fussed. And who will send their loved ones to die peacefully here now, Krishna?'

Krishna grabs Khanolkar's jaw with one hand, placing his other hand behind his neck and rhythmically moves his head from side to side, trying to loosen the muscles on his neck and upper back.

'Don't worry too much. This too shall pass,' Krishna says, jerking Khanolkar's head sideways but not hearing the anticipated click.

'Gently,' Khanolkar says.

'That *katak* sound needs to come.'

'And deflating sand trucks for no reason! What is wrong with that fool?' Khanolkar continues, 'I was a truck driver for thirty years, and if anyone tried that in my day, we would have vanished him.'

Krishna tries to crack Khanolkar's neck again but hears no click.

Flexing his fingers, Krishna prepares to tackle Khanolkar's neck yet again but is interrupted by Damayanti appearing at the door. She's on her way to the home to accompany Mala to her daily bath in the river.

'I have some news about your friend from my cousin in Kanauj.'

'Ah, good morning, Damayanti,' says Krishna, noticing the flowers in her hair.

'What news! Arrested? Hospital? Dead?' Khanolkar asks, hope glinting in his eyes.

'No, sir, nothing like that. It's unbelievable what has happened.'

'What is it?' asks a trembling Khanolkar, imagining scenes of loot and pillage, with Iyer telling everyone that he'd been fine until his ill treatment at the home in Kashi.

'Iyer Sir. He is in love!'

'Excuse me? What?' exclaimed Krishna as his hands stop kneading.

'He is in love with one Panchakanya of Benares.'

'Who is this woman? And what is this love-shove? He's over sixty-five!'

'It's impossible,' Krishna says.

'After sixty-five there is nothing! NOTHING!' Khanolkar says, gripping the sides of his chair, his knuckles strained. Releasing his shoulders, Krishna resumes the massage, trying to calm Khanolkar down with several forehead whacks expertly delivered with two index fingers.

'She is a very high caste and beautiful lady from near Kanauj. She is supposed to be very devout. He saved her from a gang of *dacoits* who were trying to kidnap her. He dedicates his exploits to her, and speaks of her with much tenderness. And who knows, maybe they will marry and have children,' Damayanti says, smiling.

Speechless, Krishna pauses the massage long enough for Khanolkar to croak, 'Oh God! Moron!'

'Sir?'

'I meant Iyer.'

'He is so romantic!' Damayanti sighs, and a tear springs from her eye, much to the amazement of Khanolkar.

'Why are you crying? Hello! What is the matter with you?'

'I am jealous.'

'Why, Damayanti?'

'Because I have never had that.'

'Be thankful for whatever you do have, Damayanti,' Khanolkar says, cruelly, looking at her acid burns.

'Khanolkar,' Krishna says sharply, appalled at his rudeness, seeing the embarrassment on Damayanti's face as she awkwardly takes her leave. Staring after her, his hands still working on Khanolkar's head, the doctor contemplates the enormity of what they have just heard.

'Iyer is in love,' Khanolkar says, his migraine now a whole battery of little cannons going off in his skull, lighting up his brain with pristine, white agony.

Krishna does not reply. Still angry at Khanolkar, he twists his neck as far as it goes, going nearly past the point of no return, but there is still no *katak*.

15

Not having seen a village in more than an hour, Iyer realises that they are in Gond territory, where the tribals still hunt among the twisted, old peepal trees. The banks shear off into ravines; the punting pole doesn't reach the riverbed any more, not even near the banks. Mountains rise up on either side of the river, dwarfing the boat, their rocky outcroppings dotted with vulture nests. Tiny caves invade the hillsides, which Iyer says are the abodes of yogis.

We could tunnel even deeper into the hills and live without ambition.

Bencho leans against the mast, depressed, his elbow and back hurting. He decides to try and catch a fish. Opening the hatch and rummaging about, he finds a piece of wood. He wraps his fishing line around it, baits the rusty hook with some leftover *roti* and lobs it into the river.

The ringing of cicadas – as shrill as machetes being sharpened on lathes – travels sharp and clear over the river. Cosmos flowers explode on the banks, long-bodied murrals splash about the reeds hunting frogs, hummingbirds dart about the riot of vegetation on the bank. The sun-sharpened turquoise sky throws light on a foot-wide ammonite fossil lying exposed on an eroded boulder, a memory of the time when the island that they now call India had inched its way across the lava mantle and crashed into the landmass of Asia, destroying the quiet lives of sea-dwelling creatures in the process.

What are human beings to rivers and mountains, sky and earth?

They pass an ascetic bathing in the shallows. He does not even glance at the boat or its passengers; the silence is broken only by the sounds of water falling off his body. There are signs of tribal life here: a campfire on the banks without discarded plastic litter, footprints in the sand that extend into an overshadowed forest – a tangle of bushes and trees. We have given a name to all of this, Iyer thinks: Ganga Maa.

Bencho gets a bite and yanks on the line. A large goonch catfish, the eater of corpses, breaks the surface next to the boat, its whiskers trembling and its shiny bony back glistening like wet armour. It shakes its head from side to side like a wet dog and breaks free of the hook. Just as Bencho reaches into the river to grab it, Iyer startles him by shouting, 'You're eating a fish when you're with a *brahmachari*?'

'Not any more, sir,' Bencho says sadly, 'your shouting made me drop it!'

'Stop fishing and come and listen.'

There are no blaring transistor radios. No truck horns in the distance.

'Pure silence,' Iyer says.

The broadening waters flow through forested islands. They would need to find the main channel again, but the river seems to flow in endless circles, the tributaries Venn diagramming each other amidst tangled islands.

Bencho baits the hook again and lobs it into the water as Iyer has his epiphany.

They pass an ancient river fort, its walls covered in creepers. A sounder of wild boar break out from a clump of lantana ahead of the boat, and paddle across the river with their heads above the surface, their bulging eyes fixed on Iyer. A flock of pintail ducks does not fly away when the boat passes them, turning instead as one organism to view the boat. Somewhere beyond the hills a tendril of smoke extends up to the skies. In time, the boat meanders between overgrown fields, jungle shrubs dotting what was once mustard or sorghum.

'They have gone to the city, these Gonds,' Iyer says, 'which makes me wonder at the weakness of their characters. The loudspeaker in Kashi said one day that they could own flats and cars. It is an insult to the sacred life, a journey towards annihilation, a rotting of the soul.'

'They want flats and cars, sir,' ventures Bencho, the line limp in his hands. 'I do too.'

'You think from the perspective of slack-jawed imbeciles in television ads. The cities are full of your Robinson Crusoes, journeying outward to capture their own islands, relocating the locals and making survivors their slaves.'

The majesty of the scene and Iyer's words are lost on the wounded Bencho, as just then a fish yanks the entire wooden block out of Bencho's hands and dives back into the river. Defeated, he leans against the mast, hitting his forehead over and over again with his palm.

'What is it, Bencho?' mocks Iyer, scouring the banks for monsters and otters, secretly hoping to find otters.

'I am thinking how long we have been on this quest to defeat Bakasura, and how I'm no closer to my political career,' he says, smacking his forehead again.

'Soon! Why are you hitting yourself?' Iyer says, watching a flock of rain quail rising out of the reeds like a burst of applause.

'I am counting the days we have been travelling by the number of times we have been beaten up.' Bencho smacks his forehead again, the sound echoing like a shot.

'So, then, how long have we been on our river?'

'About forty years I think.'

Smack.

'A *brahmachari* does not count his bruises; he collects good karma.'

'Sir, please excuse my impertinence, but where is that city you are going to win my elections in? We have fought so many battles, but you have not conquered one town. And right now we do not even know where we are. So many streams going so many places here ...'

'I am not to blame, Bencho. Bakasura has crippled the *insides* of the people here.'

'Sir, what are you talking about? The river has broken up into many. And why blame Bakasura?'

'It is more terrible than I had imagined,' Iyer says.

The boat enters a faster-flowing stretch. Iyer dozes but has trouble sleeping; Ranjana appears in his dreams like a celestial Apsara, persuading him to thrash a skeletal errand boy, running her tongue over her lips as Aurangzeb holds her from behind like a lover would, whispering into her ear.

Bencho wakes him up.

'So when, sir, are you going to introduce me to Jayachandra? He will give me a ticket if you help me persuade him.'

'Let's first destroy Bakasura lest he foil our plans, Bencho.'

'Sir, where exactly is this Bakasura? Where does he hide? Where can we find him?'

'We need silence to be able to see clearly, Bencho. We need the absence of noise for any great quest,' Iyer declares, sitting up.

'Sir?'

'To find a great demon like Bakasura, we have to avoid making a noise. We need to be guided. God does not scream into our ears, Bencho. See how these trees grow. See how the fish live. They do so in silence. The sun, moon and stars are silent. No matter how you argue with them, they will respond with silence. When you are young they are silent, and when you are about to die they will still be silent. And after our factories have drunk the rivers and burnt the trees and we have poisoned the fish, there will still be silence. And in that desolation, it will still speak to us. That is God. To find Bakasura, Bencho, we need to listen very carefully.'

'But life is always noisy, sir. Like our Kashi!'

'"Kashi" means to listen. Now do you understand? Remember to listen.'

'How do you know, sir?' Bencho asks, straining at the oars.

'When I sleep, I travel to that dimension when Bhīma lived on this earth and relive all those creatures he destroyed. We are locked to those we have encountered. They become a part of our destinies, Bencho.'

'Where did you get your power to do this? And where is this other dimension?'

'No matter what you think with your five senses, the world is as it is. Consider yourself blessed, Bencho. We *brahmacharis* have to deal with so much more than mortals like you.'

An eagle with a hilsa fish in its claws flies over the boat, its shadow making Iyer look skyward. It lands on its nest high up in a mango tree, causing a langur to jump off a branch and into the foliage. The eagle rips into the still-gasping fish, dropping chunks of its flesh into a chick's open beak.

'Sir, your life experience is different from us humans? How sir?'

'Bencho, the human embryo resembles a fish at one stage. At other times it has a yolk sac just like a bird's egg, and then it develops a tail like a monkey. So we were many things once upon a time. We have plenty of life experience.'

'So, why do you only dream of that time when you were Bhīma? What about the other lives? Why not a fish dream, sir?'

'Yes, why not the migration of a hilsa fish that migrates upriver to the place where it was spawned once upon a time? I can see us now, swimming up the Ganges ...'

'Sir, what if someone were to catch and eat us? We have passed so many gill nets this journey, and the holes in the nets are not large enough for the smallest minnows to escape.' Bencho grins, enjoying the conversation now.

'Yes, Bencho. In the olden days hilsa was not caught between Lakshmi *puja* and Saraswati *puja,* to let them breed and replenish the river. But times have changed. We have succumbed to the Christians, and the first chapter of their book that says they believe they were given dominion over the earth and its creatures. The world is not our home, they tell themselves. Heaven is our home and that is why they do not care so much for the forests and its beings. We Indians have learned this from them. We are no longer a part of the world; we think we are its masters, to eat as we wish and fear that if we do not keep up with the rest, the barbarians will enslave us again. That is the great fear we have. The whole world lives with this fear, holding it close to their hearts as they run towards the precipice.'

'I would not mind some hilsa, actually.'

'We have forgotten what the sages tell us: that all life is one long creature stretched out through time and space, living, dying, decaying and growing simultaneously, each aspect a part of the rest – tied to humanity, tied to who we are now and then and later. Our festivals came with the change of seasons, the harvest and the solstices, to prepare us for what earth and time would give us. Now instead of celebrations for the soul, our festivals have become celebrations for shopping. We drink the holy river – it gives life to our crops, and when we eat, it becomes our body. The river becomes *us*. Once we never painted Ganesh idols before immersion. Now we paint them with poisons and your hilsa floats up asphyxiated.'

'Hilsa is very nice with mustard, sir. I do not wish to be reborn a fish,' says Bencho.

Iyer begins to sing the *Sree Ragam*, an ode to the Ganges and other holy rivers.

Om Gangeca Yamune caiva Godavari Saraswati
Narmade Sindhu Kaveri jalesmin samnidhim kuru.

Hail O ye Ganges, Yamuna, Godavari, Saraswati,
Narmada, Sindhu and Kaveri, come and approach
these waters.

They reach a portion of the river with many small islands, each filled with migratory waterfowl, the cacophony of their honking and squawking coming to them through breaks in the wind like the sounds of a distant city. And they journey on until human settlement invades their reveries in the form of blaring Bollywood music.

Bencho punts the boat to the banks and buys some spinach and a bag of broken rice from a woman with a large goitre and tattoos on her arms. They make their way further downstream, coming to another industrial area where factories and tanneries line the banks, waste pouring into the water from crowded shanties. A mangy dog feeds on a woman's bloated corpse by the water's edge, scanning the horizon for competition; further along an old woman squats in a rubbish dump and lifts her sari to move her bowels. An island of polystyrene floats past them. Shrouded figures pass on the bank towards a cremation ghat, holding a stretcher bearing a corpse. The sight arouses a restless foreboding in Iyer, who stands up and chants to the river, his arms extended and eyes closed,

Om Namah Shivaya!
Om Namah Shivaya!
Om Namah Shivaya!

His chant is broken by a splash; Iyer sees Bencho throwing a plastic packet of rubbish into the river. Leaning outwards, he picks it up and flings it back into the boat. Upset, he turns to Bencho.

'How can I live truly when one sees clearly the inherent darkness of existence within your own self? Such irony for the speakers of truth, to know that they themselves are in need of rescue. Such irony, to know that your own *chela* pollutes the river of truth.'

'Sir, it is only a small packet.'

'"Sir, it is only a small packet."' Iyer mimics, the veins on his neck standing out. 'We worship the gods of the forest but chop the trees. Progress, Bencho! This is what we call progress,' Iyer splutters. 'Tell that to the river!' he bellows.

'Sir, I will become vegetarian I think, in time. I will leave the hilsa alone,' Bencho says guiltily.

But Iyer doesn't hear him, having spotted a man defecating near the bank.

'Bastard, don't shit in the Ganges!' he yells.

Other heads emerge from the reeds around him.

'Sir, but you just said the river was a part of us,' Bencho says, leaning into the oars.

'The best parts only,' Iyer snaps, looking for missiles to hurl.

The man curses and tries to frog-hop backwards into safety.

'Go shit in your father's field, insect!' yells Iyer, throwing a rotten *brinjal* at the man, missing him by inches.

'All fields lead to the river, you mad dog,' the man yells, flinging the *brinjal* back at Iyer.

'And all rivers go to the sea, so shit in the Bay of Bengal,' shouts Bencho, punting away as Iyer hurls the boat's collected rubbish at them, delighted that someone else was getting flak for destroying the river.

They float away, and Bencho is taken aback by the sight of an upright rhesus macaque walking along the bank, like a relic from ancient times when men did not exist, and the apes were the kings of the earth.

16

In time, the boat finds the main channel, the speed of the flow increases and Bencho uses the pole to push the boat away from rocks as they career downriver. When it slows down, they find enormous boulders littering the river and surrounding countryside as if they had just fallen from the sky. It is the ruins of a city, as can be seen from the stone pillars jutting out of the riverbanks.

'Who were these people who once lived here?' asks Bencho.

'I do not know,' replies Iyer.

'Why did they leave? What happened?' asks Bencho as they pass the shell of what would once have been an elephant stable. On an island of grass, in the crushed remains of an unrecognisable statue, crows pick at a large dead masheer fish.

'One day in the future, when the ashes of our civilization have been blown about by the wind, the survivors will look at our ruins the same way we look at these ruins now.'

'Sir, it will only get better, I feel. Once upon a time there were only fields here, and all the people could do was dig and plant things. Back-breaking work. Now we have factories, and soon we will have a car for every family,' Bencho says, repeating the election speech he had heard in Varanasi. 'When I am a politician I will make sure that everyone has a car, a flat and ...We should head to Kanauj now. Why are we meandering like this?'

'Soon, Bencho.'

'Jayachandra won't be able to say no if a big man like you introduces me, sir: Brahmin, good family, good English.'

'There is savagery at the beginning of the ascent of a civilisation,' Iyer begins, 'then a glorious flowing into learning and science, and then, of course, the decadence and sloth that lead to destruction from within and without. We are locked in this – the defeated of today becoming the victors of tomorrow. And then the next civilisation will write books about us, not seeing that it is, all the while, hurtling towards the same fate.'

'But what stage are we at, sir? India, that is.'

'We have to transcend our curses and wounds and discover who we truly are.'

'Sir, I get cursed every day. Sometimes, several times a day. I do not believe in curses. Just last month Khanolkar cursed me to be reborn as a cockroach.'

A spluttering barge travelling upriver chugs into view and interrupts their conversation. They see a boat filled with rows of men in handcuffs, with two policemen – armed with Enfield rifles – on guard. This can't be good, thinks Bencho.

'Row alongside it, Bencho. Row along their boat NOW,' Iyer hisses with pursed lips, raising his staff for emphasis.

'No, sir. No. They are the police!'

Iyer seems to see sense for a moment before the barge's engine splutters and stops, its exhaust spluttering out a plume of black smoke – much to Iyer's joy.

'The gods have decided for us,' says Iyer, and Bencho breaks out in a cold sweat.

'No, sir, please.'

The engine box rattling, the barge turns with loud instructions from one of the constables to the boatman, and pulls up at a reed bed on a small island.

Separated by about thirty feet of water, Iyer cups his hands to shout, 'I am Bhīma of Benares, *brahmachari!*

Bencho rolls his eyes heavenwards.

'What are these men in chains for?' he continues.

'The roads are closed and they all have a special date to get to!' the constable shouts back.

'What are they guilty of?' Iyer asks

'Get lost,' says a constable, unzipping himself at the stern.

Iyer shouts to a chubby man in a well-stitched shirt, handcuffed in the last row.

'What are you in chains for, man?'

'Eh?'

'What are you in chains for, man?' he bellows.

The man thinks for a few seconds and grins.

'Sir, I am here only because of poverty.'

'Poverty?'

'I did not have enough to bribe the police when I was caught.' The other convicts snigger.

Bencho's only form of protest is refusing to row the boat up to the barge, but it floats closer towards them anyway.

The man next to him is short, with a Hitler moustache. 'What are you here for?' Iyer asks him.

'I am here because I am too gentle, sir.'

'Gentle?'

'Yes, I could not bear the slaps of the policeman and said I did it, sir.'

'Did what?'

'Fell into the arms of a beautiful girl, but they said she was unwilling,' he smirks, tossing his head while the rest of the convicts snigger again.

A clean-shaven convict with a row all to himself raises his hand, and the whole boat falls silent. He's tall and wiry, with pale skin and sharp, intelligent eyes. A long scar runs from his forehead to his ear, passing through an eyelid, healed but distended.

'And you? What is your tale of suffering?'

The two boats are now close enough for the tyres that hang off the side of the barge to touch the boat.

'My dear, I am here for the crime of falling in love,' he says smiling, the scar turning pink as he does so.

'Falling in love?'

'I love what I do, my dear, and that is why I am here. People call me "The Lover".'

'And what do you do?'

'I remove all that inhibit progress,' he says evenly. No one laughs; they look away, keen to not involve themselves in the exchange.

'And you?' he asks a tattooed Adivasi sitting handcuffed and quiet at the rear of the boat. The man turns to look at Iyer, revealing a bruised face and broken teeth. He says nothing.

'Don't ask him, my dear, he has lost his voice,' The Lover remarks, looking at the other convicts, who guffaw immediately.

Standing to his full height, Iyer speaks: 'I am Bhīma of Benares, *brahmachari*! I took an oath to uphold justice. I grant you all release.'

For a few seconds no one replies, and all that can be heard is the sound of the river, except for the sounds of Bencho hurriedly trying to cover his body with the tarpaulin.

'Shut up, you madman. Get lost,' the constable shouts.

'Sir, I have interrogated these men and I find them innocent!' Iyer continues.

'Fool. Do you even know who they are? What they are?'

'Fool? You call the Bhīma a fool? I command you to release these innocents. Or you will feel my mace across your pitiful face.'

'I, Constable Vikas, command you to fuck off! Before I shove this *lathi* up your arse,' he says, spitting into the river to emphasise his point.

With a loud cry Iyer leaps onto the barge, swinging his staff wildly at the stunned constable, who steps backwards, grasping at his side for his ancient Lee Enfield rifle, which looks like it's seen better days. Seeing his chance, The Lover gets up and, with a swift elbow jab, shoves the constable into the river. The other constable, who has never worked a rifle before, is trying frantically but unsuccessfully to draw the bolt, when it is twisted out of his grasp by another member of the gang. Within minutes, four men have divested the constable of his keys, bashed him about a few times and tossed him into the river.

They swim away as far as they can, trying to dodge the chains being flung at them from the barge.

'Victory!' Iyer shouts, while the convicts cheer him on wildly, slapping him on the back as Iyer raises his hands to the heavens.

Seeing The Lover picking up the rifle and raising it in the direction of the swimming constabulary, Iyer snatches it from him.

'Let them go,' he pleads, 'they are our brothers too.'

'Listen here, my dear,' The Lover says with exquisitely gentle menace, delicately placing a hand on Iyer's shoulder, 'you've helped us so you get one chance from me. I will give you one chance. Now, you mind your own business,' he says, abruptly moving his hand from shoulder to throat and squeezing. Iyer gasps for breath and falls to his knees.

'Please leave him be,' comes a tremulous voice, and Bencho appears from beneath the tarpaulin, trembling with fear and partly wishing he had remained hidden.

The constables have reached the other bank and run into the forest.

The Lover softens and releases Iyer, grinning at Bencho.

'Sorry, grandpa. I guess I do owe you. You can come with us. I have a politician friend downstream who'll help us.'

'Why would I come with you?' Iyer rasps, still on the floor of the boat, rubbing his throat.

'We fight for freedom,' The Lover says romantically. 'No one dares enter our area.'

'No thank you, Mr Lover. I will respectfully refuse your offer but, if you don't mind, I have a request.'

Unsure of what to make of Iyer, The Lover listens.

'I ask just one favour. Go to the beautiful lady Panchakanya of Benares, and tell her I did this for her. She's the divine light of my life.'

There's an amazed silence on the boat, broken by The Lover, who laughs in amazement. Hearing him, the rest of the convicts start whooping too.

'OK. Right,' says The Lover in patently mocking tones.

'Sir, I freed you. Can you not do this one small thing for me?'

'You made us throw two constables into the river, and that is a criminal case. Attempted murder! If you'd let me get rid of them we would not have that on our heads. The district magistrate is my cousin. I would have been released in a few weeks anyway, but now I've got to worry about this new charge!'

'Darkness cannot free darkness, only light can do that. What you put out into the world, you receive back. Is that not true?'

'Oh, you're an educated fellow, are you? Lording it over us, are you? You'd better be careful, or we'll finish you off right now.'

'We're all brothers here,' says Iyer, finally concerned that the situation may not go as well as he'd hoped.

'I killed my brother,' one of the convicts says, to guffaws from the rest of them.

'Start the engine,' The Lover says. 'Shut up and get lost now, old man,' he says, all playfulness vanished.

'But you must listen to me. I am …' Suddenly a convict punches Iyer, and another leaps on Bencho, pushing him down. Iyer stumbles and is punched again. Picking up a rifle, The Lover nonchalantly strikes Iyer across the forehead with the butt, with a sound like an axe hitting a coconut. Iyer falls backwards into the shallows, the taste of metal filling his mouth, the sky darkening as his eyes close.

When he comes to, he's still in the water and Bencho has his arms around him, holding his head above the water. Bencho is sobbing, his salty tears stinging a bleeding cut on Iyer's forehead.

'Don't cry, Bencho,' he says weakly, the sound of the barge now distant.

'Sir,' Bencho shouts, crying harder from relief.

'Please don't cry,' he says again.

With consciousness comes the pain, shooting down the side of his face. Iyer cries out.

'Bastards,' Bencho mutters, his teeth clenched.

'My friends! My friends! I freed you.'

Bencho starts pushing him through the water and towards the boat, which has run into some dead branches trailing over the water like a broken spider's web.

17

'There is no hope. The beaten of today will become the beaters of tomorrow. There is no end,' moans Bencho, a cloud of mosquitoes buzzing like a halo around his head, adding to his misery. He gets Iyer into the boat, propping him against the mast.

The pain from Iyer's broken tooth throbs with every heartbeat, and spreads past his jaw to his neck and shoulders. His ribs ache from the punches and hurt with every breath. Leaning against the mast, he watches mosquitoes settle on his skin and feed, unmolested. Iyer has a vision of himself blowing on a conch rallying the troops, the veins on his neck bulging with the effort. *Fight. Fight. Fight.*

'Bencho! Are you with me? I watch my words from a long way off. It is like they belong to someone else,' he groans, pressing his head against the mast, the wound on his forehead weeping onto the wood.

'Maybe this is a bad dream. We will wake up soon, sir.'

'Am I dreaming my wounds, Bencho?' Iyer asks, touching his forehead and wincing, the vision dissipating, 'or do these wounds dream me?'

'I am tired of the beating and also sometimes of your wisdom, sir. Please stop,' begs Bencho, his swollen face slick with tears that keep on coming.

'It is a slight setback,' Iyer says, pausing to spit out blood. 'All is secondary to divine providence.'

'Sir, you are like a fool with your actions but a wise man in your philosophy. Why, sir?'

Iyer looks at his hands as if they hold a clue, but sees only bruises and smudges of blood. 'I am the residue of all my ancestors as we move backwards into time, and so on and on and on, until that which happened in the sludge at the bottom of swamps with writhing creatures – unholy things, terrible things – is also a part of me.'

'OK!' Bencho says, exasperated, raising one hand for Iyer to stop. He grabs the pole and starts punting the boat away from the bank. This man wasn't a great thinker who was going to kick off his political career; he was a maniac.

'All time happens at once, Bencho.'

Bencho transfers his frustration to a mosquito on his forearm, which he slaps with such vigour that the sting hurts more than a bite would have. He looks at Iyer with something bordering on disdain.

'I do not know where my rages come from, Bencho,' Iyer says, dropping his head. 'But when I watch myself charge, it makes sense. A man must obey his own law. A life has to follow its own course.'

'Course?'

'Somewhere else in space and time I sat cowering, a boot on my neck, my hands joined in supplication during the Battle of Talikota – if my divine memory holds true. That has passed now. This too shall pass, Bencho. Have faith.'

'Faith? In what? How can God let you be attacked by people you helped?' Bencho asks, pulverising a mosquito and wondering – just like the mosquito – why, indeed, a God would unleash such monsters upon the faithful.

'God is much better and much worse than that. Who says God is good?' Iyer's tooth rings with a fresh wave of pain, as if to prove this point. 'The pain we feel is the divine accompaniment to the task at hand. Think of it as a song. Try singing, Bencho, that is what I do when the suffering is too much. But not a film song, or I will vomit.'

'I will leave you at your brother's house. And I will sing for now, though if I sing I will start crying, sir,' Bencho says, losing the riverbed with the pole and pulling it back into the boat. Sitting down, he starts to sing.

Suddenly tilting his head, Bencho freezes. 'Where are the oars?' Bencho asks, looking about.

'I don't know,' Iyer replies, going through his sodden pockets, trying to remember if he'd brought any Crocin with him.

'Why does this happen to us, sir?' Bencho cries, looking for the oars under the floorboards, and realising that they must have got lost somehow in the earlier fracas. Perhaps they slid out of the boat?

'Why can't we succeed once? Just once?'

'Don't worry, Bencho, you will become a politician very soon,' Iyer says, scouring his pockets again and finding nothing.

'Really, sir?'

Iyer does not miss the sarcasm.

'Lord Krishna told me so. He is with us on our journey.'

'Where did you see him?' Bencho asks. 'Couldn't he have kept an eye on the oars earlier?'

'I saw him in my dreams.'

'Where are the oars?' Bencho repeats, louder this time, searching the river bottom with the punting pole again, not finding the silt again.

'I don't know, Bencho. But have faith, Ganga Maa will always take us to where we are headed.' And saying so, Iyer put his head in his hands.

They float along in silence. Bencho, grateful that the stove is still on board, starts preparing spinach, cooking it to mush so that Iyer's teeth can withstand it. The river grows so wide that he cannot see the banks any more. Comforted by the smell of food, Bencho dozes off.

He dreams of another boat. It is a much larger one which both he and Iyer row. Other men sit alongside, also rowing, pulling on long oars and cursing. Iyer has only one arm. Grinning, he tries to attach an oar to his stump, clicking it into place.

Click.

Click.

Bencho wakes up to see Iyer holding the Major's gun, the cylinder clicking as it rotates.

'Where did you get that?' he asks startled, springing upright.

'An old friend gave it to me,' Iyer says, spinning the cylinder again.

'Sir. Give it to me. Please,' says Bencho, forcing a smile.

'The world may deprive a man of life, but it cannot deprive him of death,' Iyer says, sounding like his old assured self.

'Sir, enough philosophy. Give me the gun,' Bencho says, all traces of sleep obliterated by horror-driven adrenaline.

'All it will take to send me back to the heavens is a little pressure from this finger.' Iyer raises the revolver to his temple, pulling the hammer back with his thumb.

'Sir. You must give me the gun,' Bencho says, his mouth dry.

'Why?'

'We have not finished what we set out to do. We have not filed for my corporator seat and you have not ...'

'There is nothing wrong in choosing release, Bencho. They tell us that suicide is cowardly, when it is quite obvious that there is nothing in the world to which every man is more entitled to than his own life. Many a great sage has meditated until he has released himself from the world.'

'I will wait until you release yourself with meditation, but please give me your gun. What about your family? Your brothers, their children ... how will they feel?'

Iyer looks out over the water, still holding the gun to his head.

'Let's go and see them. They would love to see you, no? You can tell the children about your adventures. They're downstream, aren't they, in the village near the paper plant? No?'

'Yes.'

'The gun, sir.'

Bencho looks hard at Iyer, who stares back at him. The moment Iyer lowers his hand, he snatches the gun and throws it overboard. 'What do you care, Bencho?' he asks.

'About what?'

'About me shooting myself.'

'You are my guru, sir, and my friend.'

Iyer starts to say something but thinks better of it.

'I am the guru who will help you with your nomination so you can become a corporator who loots people? Politicians have no morals, Bencho, not in this country.'

'No sir. I have morals,' Bencho replies, adding, '*And* my country *is* great. *We* must be proud.'

'What pride is there in being Indian?' Iyer asks angrily. 'We are the lowest of the low, the most piteous, servile slaves that have ever lived in the history of humanity. We are the armpit of Asia. We have had the boot on our neck these last five hundred years. Nothing has changed. No one respects us. We don't respect ourselves.'

'Sir, we chased the British out,' Bencho says, taken aback by Iyer's criticism of the motherland.

'Chased? Who told you that? The British were looters. What does that make us when so many of us were ruled by a few looters? We were too busy molesting the peasants to fight back. The Mohammedans were no different, except that they liked chopping off heads. When Vijayanagara fell, all was lost. We are still recovering. Then we replaced those looters with bigger looters.'

'We had Gandhiji, sir,' Bencho says quietly. 'Remember, one old man booted out the powerful British.'

'The deification of that crackpot Karamchand is one of the main reasons for our intellectual gutter today. If he were born in any other time, his bald head would have been a decoration on a gate spike. Karamchand was a suitable boy for the West because we aren't supposed to fight the white man. They've used him to make villains of anyone who rightly used force against the looters,' Iyer fumes.

'Sir, listen …'

'No, Bencho, I know exactly what people like you think. That he is above criticism, well …'

'No, sir, listen. Well, yes, that too, but LISTEN!'

A faint roaring can be heard in the distance, ahead of the river's next bend. It is the sound of water, muted but full of terrible promise.

'It's a waterfall, sir!' Bencho says, his eyes wide with fear. 'And we have no oars!'

The sound grows clearer as the boat approaches it, the roar growing deafening as, turning the bend, the waterfall comes into sight: a plume of vapour rising into the heavens a kilometre downstream.

Iyer takes the pole as the boat enters the rapids, dirty whitecaps filling a brown river. The boat hits some rocks, nearly capsizing it, but slides back into the water. It careens along, Bencho sobbing with fear, with his head pressed against the mast. Iyer begins singing at the top of his voice.

Pachai ma malai pol meni. Oorile kaani illai uravu martoruvar illai
Paaril nin paadhamoolam patrine paramamoorthy.

I have no place; no properties; no relatives; none other than you
I have got hold of your lotus feet, o Lord of the universe.

The boat enters the rapids. Seeing rocks ahead, Bencho tries to use the pole to push it away, but it gets wedged between two boulders and snaps in two. With superhuman effort, he steers the way with the half-pole, trying to reach the banks until that, too, is snatched from his hands by the raging cataract.

Shouting in fear and throwing himself at the bottom of the boat, Bencho grabs onto the mast as the boat hurtles towards the chasm, completely out of their control.

Karolee vannnane en kannnane kadaarugindren
Paaril nin paadhamoolam patrine paramamoorthy.

O Krishna, you are my only refuge, I am crying for
salvation at your feet
I have got hold of your lotus feet, o Lord of the
universe.

A mist rises like smoke, marked by shimmering rainbows.

'We're going to be dashed on the rocks!' Bencho shouts, cowering in the boat.

'It is only death. Do not fear,' Iyer shouts back, reaching across and taking Bencho's hand and holding it firmly. The boat crashes to a halt, shuddering against a rock, teetering at the edge of the waterfall. Iyer looks into the mist rising from the river some fifteen feet below, and has a vision.

He is carrying a butcher's cleaver – the kind that needs daily sharpening and goes black in the monsoon. He runs through a battle between British redcoats and Indian sepoys, everyone fighting hand to hand around him. Corpses float downriver. A blonde child of about ten, dressed in a dirty white smock, runs through the shallows, her hair in disarray, catching the sunlight. She looks at Iyer and begins to sob.

The vision passes. He opens his eyes and sees Bencho with his eyes closed tight against the spray, his brows furrowed in prayer.

Three cormorants fly over the river in formation, their heads turning from side to side as if they're looking for something. Iyer sees them and feels a calmness descend over him. He sees himself as if he's floating over the boat with them, and closes his eyes.

The boat dislodges and plunges into the chasm.

18

Cutting into the depths of the water, the boat goes completely underwater for a second before it rockets back up to the surface, its hull leaking like a sieve. Iyer and Bencho clasp the mast, disoriented and knee-deep in water. The vessel is pushed out into a vast stillness, a speck in the midst of a bankless lake, leaning to one side again.

Exhausted and surprised at their survival, Bencho drops anchor. He has hit his knee hard against the boat and it aches, but he is alive, so it hardly matters. He finds a length of bamboo floating in the lake and retrieves it to use as a punting pole. They bail the water out from under the deck with the dish and a coconut shell, dazed into silence. The clouds disperse, and the sky turns azure.

Setting their clothes out to dry, they lie down next to them on the deck, letting the sunshine fall on their aching bodies, Iyer shivering in spite of the warmth. He turns in his sleep and winces, finding his face swollen and a pain throbbing from his tooth outwards to his jaw and skull. Iyer sleeps intermittently, eyes scrunched against the light, but waking up now and then to the familiar sight of Bencho on board. He loses track of time. At some point, he feels the grip of his fever lessening, and opens his eyes without being dazzled by daylight. Cotton-mouthed and heavy-headed, he starts to sit up.

Bencho helps him up, relieved to see him capable of movement.

'Happy Holi, sir,' he says, daubing Iyer with a symbolic finger of colour. 'Got some at the last village while you were sleeping, but they had no medicine. We are close to your brother's village, I think.'

Touching Iyer's forehead, he sees that he is still fevered, but not burning up like before. The swelling of his jaw is about the same. Iyer falls asleep again.

Singing from the riverbank awakens Iyer. He looks at the people milling further down the bank. He sees two women washing Holi colour off their faces, squatting in the shallows.

'I know this place, Bencho,' Iyer says, looking around. 'This is my home.'

'In this life, sir?'

Iyer tries to put on his jacket, finding the simple task surprisingly challenging.

Looking at the two women on the bank, Iyer smiles.

'My brother, he has sent two princesses to greet me. What a fine gesture.'

'They're only village girls, sir,' Bencho says with a snort. 'I don't like this place,' he adds, seeing a flaming pyre further down the bank, surrounded by buffaloes eating ash on the cremation ground.

Painfully, Iyer stands.

'Princesses! Princesses!' Iyer shouts as best as he can in his diminished state. 'I am Bhīma of Kashi. If you all are in need of a *brahmachari* to protect you all from lascivious males, just say the word, and I will die protecting you!'

'Thank you, kind *baba*,' says one of the girls, joining her hands together solemnly before dissolving into a giggling fit.

Bencho docks the boat on the bank, tying it securely to a tree. They walk towards the village, Iyer leaning on Bencho, head drooping, and Bencho dragging his foot, his knee swollen.

In the village square, a group of mill workers are constructing a giant effigy of the demoness Putna. Another group drapes fairy lights and banners on the Ferris wheel set up behind the demoness. A group of children shoot long streams of coloured water at each other as yet more workers set up hoardings around the Ferris wheel.

'A man has come in a boat. He claims he is a *brahmachari*, and an incarnation of Lord Bhīma,' one of the giggling girls tells the mill workers as Iyer and Bencho enter.

Iyer bows to the people in the courtyard, not without effort, as his back aches terribly.

'Ah Bhīmaji! Come play some cards with us,' grins a mill worker, exposing rotten teeth flecked with tobacco.

The mustached village constable gets up and limps towards the duo.

'You know why I drag this leg?'

'Sir, why?' asks Bencho.

'Because it has been overused from kicking good-for-nothing vagabonds out of the village,' the constable says, looking at Bencho with great intent. Surviving thus far has given Bencho courage, though, and he finds that he doesn't care any more.

'Sir, you know why I drag my leg?' he asks.

'No.'

'Dog shit. Twenty feet back.' Bencho shows the constable the underside of his shoe and salutes him at the same time.

The constable steps forward and grabs Bencho's collar with one hand and Iyer's with the other, for good measure. Pain screams up his swollen jaw, and he tries ineffectually to lift his staff. Pushing Bencho to one side, the constable raises his fist above Iyer's broken face, and is about to bring it down on him when he is interrupted by a gleaming white SUV lighting the scene up with its glaring headlights. The constable blinks and unhands Iyer, who falls to the floor.

The car door opens and a tall, trim man emerges, followed by a blast of frozen air. He carries the mark of his caste on his forehead and is impeccably dressed in a spotless white shirt and slacks.

'What is going on here!' he says.

'Abhishek Sir, vagrants,' the constable says ingratiatingly.

The man looks at Iyer carefully.

'This man?'

'Yes, sir. He could be a pickpocket or even a *dacoit*. But don't worry, sir, I am taking care of him.' The constable bends down and takes Iyer by the collar again.

'Stop, Rohit,' says Abhishek, and the constable freezes. He bends over and lends Iyer a hand to help him up.

'To what do we owe the pleasure of this visit, dear Uncle?'

'Cannot a travelling *brahmachari* come to meet his dearest brother?' Iyer asks, Abhishek swimming before his eyes.

'The home told us of your escape.' Abhishek says, smirking.

'Escape? I was not in jail!' Iyer says, anger clearing his head. He draws himself up to his full height, but still cannot quite reach his nephew's nose.

'Welcome, Uncle,' Abhishek says in a tone that is far from warm. 'I will inform Father and we will prepare a room for you.'

Seeing Bencho, he says, 'Is he with you?'

'Yes. He goes where I go, dear nephew.'

'There is room for him in the servants' quarters,' Abhishek says.

'I will arrange my own accommodation,' Iyer says. 'You may tell your father that we shall come for breakfast.'

'We?'

'Yes, we.'

'OK. OK, Uncle. Eight. Don't be late,' Abhishek says, heading towards his SUV. The constable rushes ahead to open the door for him, and then looks at Iyer, confused as to how to treat him. True, he is Abhishek Sir's uncle, but that was not a loving familial exchange. Still, why should he involve himself in the matter of family? Best to be on the safe side; tomorrow they could be all pally again and it would be remembered that a mere constable had been insolent with a member of the Iyer family.

'Sir,' he says to Iyer, 'you should have told me. Is there anything I can do?'

'Good man,' says Iyer, 'can you find a place for myself and my friend to spend the night?'

He can barely get the words out due to the pain in his tooth.

'Sir, yes, sir,' the constable replies, 'if it is not too uncomfortable for you, there is the buffalo shed.'

'It will be fine,' Iyer says, now feeling faint.

'Ay, Mooga,' the constable calls to a boy herding buffalo, 'take these gentlemen to the stables, they will spend the night there.'

The boy nods and waves to Iyer and Bencho to follow him.

'I am so tired, child,' he whispers; the boy hums the tune of the sentence in reply.

'Make way. Make way.' The constable shouts as the buffalo boy leads the duo to the shed, singing a song made up of noises and not words.

The shed is a long structure with urns of grain stacked along the edges. On one side, a row of buffaloes are tied up for milking. On the other side, fodder is piled up to the rafters, where a small platform has been built.

Iyer sits down on a charpoy, closing his eyes in relief.

'Ah! Finally to be in a castle. I have stayed in many castles, Bencho, but this one is particularly magnificent,' Iyer says as Bencho helps him undress.

Sanctuary.

Mooga returns a while later carrying rags, a mug of warm water, a bottle of Dettol and a bottle of iodine, which he hands to Bencho. Leaving, he returns again with two tumblers of milk, some chapattis, a coarse military blanket and some sheets.

'Bless you, child,' Iyer says, welling up at the extraordinary joy of receiving a simple act of kindness.

Bencho pours a capful of Dettol into the mug of water and starts wiping down Iyer's bruises. Iyer's body is skeletal: skin stretched across his bones, every muscle defined.

When Mooga returns an hour later, he herds the buffaloes into the shed. After he ties them in their stalls, he climbs onto a platform in the rafters and stares at them from his perch.

'Rest, sir, rest. You'll be with your family soon. And I will return to Kashi tomorrow' says Bencho.

'I have to find this Bakasura, Bencho. Ah, my tooth!' Iyer groans, feeling as if his body might disintegrate.

'Bakasura can wait. You're home.'

'The heavens have forgotten me.'

A big, bright moon has risen. Mooga on the rafters opens a pouch tied around his neck, from which he takes out a round ball of opium. Rolling it further into a smaller ball, he comes down from the platform and offers it to Iyer.

Iyer smiles in gratitude but turns it down, explaining that he does not believe in narcotics.

Bencho takes it and crumbles some into Iyer's glass of milk when Iyer's back is turned. Bencho eats the rest gratefully, popping it into his mouth and swallowing it whole.

Staring at the flickering fireflies, with the occasional snort from the buffaloes, a warmth envelops Iyer and Bencho as they plummet into a dreamless, opium-heavy sleep.

The next morning, Iyer wakes up before dawn to the sounds of buffaloes being milked by the boy. His toothache is still panging, but it's nothing like the agony of the night before.

Beside his bed, Iyer sees cloves, milk, Brufen tablets and turmeric powder. When he attempts to pay Mooga for these kindnesses, he shakes his head, refusing.

Refreshed, Iyer follows the buffaloes down to a pond near the river. The wound on his forehead is beginning to heal, and the Brufen and cloves have allowed him to forget his jaw for the moment.

Butterflies have congregated on the sand – shimmering kaleidescopes where the buffaloes have urinated. Sunlight catches the wings of thousands of damselflies as they flash and hover over the water, hunting the butterflies.

Using the steps by the temple, Iyer descends into the bathing area by the river and washes his dhoti in the shade of a peepal tree. He uses the wet corner of his dhoti to clean the stains on his jacket, and a washing stone to beat out the mud caked into the sleeves. After he is done, he sits navel-deep in the water and washes himself, feeling the river embracing him like a living entity.

A spider descends on him and floats about his head, buffeted by invisible winds. Opening his eyes, he watches it swing across his view like a trapeze artist, its single thread catching the light.

Iyer prays.

He does not look towards the sky or the middle distance; instead he stares down into the water, his eyes blurring out the surface. He imagines the river flowing through him – as if he were a sieve – washing away the fragility of his body and leaving behind a purified shell. He breathes deep, letting his lungs fill with air, emptying his mind of thoughts, focusing on his breath, using his *pranayama* to commune with the deities: his equals – he feels – both in divinity and degradation, suspended, like him, in the infinite darkness of being.

19

So I return.

His clothes, folded in a plastic packet in his backpack and kept under the floorboards of the boat, are miraculously dry. Bencho brings him a clean shirt and dhoti, and gets a fresh shirt for himself. Bencho's swollen knee has gone down a bit by now, and he feels more like his old, cheerful self.

'Sir, you are looking top class,' he says, beaming at the thought of a hot breakfast waiting for him. Mooga offers Iyer a bowl of frothy milk, fresh from that morning's milking, miming that Iyer should drink it.

'An angel, Bencho,' Iyer says, smiling at Mooga. 'He is an angel sent to ease our way.' Iyer accepts the milk and takes a deep draught without noticing the flecks of opium in it.

'One must not say no to an angel's offerings,' he says, handing Mooga back the bowl.

The festival of Holi is in full swing outside the buffalo shed. Children and adults alike run this way and that, spraying people with large water syringes. Most people are high on *bhang*. A few young men wait for an opportunity to shoot coloured water at passing women, and more so for a chance to cop a feel 'by accident', as today is a day when they may be able to get away with it without being slapped in return.

'Come, it is time!' Iyer says, flinging open the shed door and eyeing the streets warily.

Iyer has a problem. He needs to make it to his family home looking presentable, because Tamil Brahmins celebrate Holi on a different day altogether, and he is about to enter a sombre family gathering where he knows they'll be washed and starched as always. Feeling the opium blossoming in his veins like a sunflower, Iyer has an idea.

'Run!'

Adjusting his collar, combing his beard and smoothing his hair down for the last time, Iyer bolts from the stable door, Bencho in pursuit. They are immediately spotted and chased by a group of children. Though Iyer is exerting himself, he feels like he's floating – his legs moving of their own accord.

'Get them,' shouts a sour-faced girl, magenta from head to foot, and her cohorts train their *pichkaris* on the two men. Bencho ducks into an alley, but Iyer runs ahead, spotting a large white cow. He ducks behind it as the children fire, its white side going pink as the blast of colour hits it. Snorting in surprise, the cow bucks, scattering the children. Iyer thanks it and races on, the pain in his bad knee returning as he approaches his brother's home, just ahead: modest, serene, clean. For a moment, it's as if he has just returned to it from a trip to the market. Home.

Bencho is nowhere to be seen. Unlatching the low gate, Iyer walks up to the door and takes a deep breath. As he reaches for the doorbell, the sour-faced girl springs up from behind the rhododendrons, holding her plunger full of mangeta dye.

'No!' cries Iyer, trapped between the girl and the door.

Iyer raises his hands in silent entreaty as the girl stares at him, raising and aiming the plunger. At that very moment, Bencho hurtles through space towards her, sending her flying into the bushes. Getting to his feet, Bencho picks up the *pichkari* and empties it on the stunned child's face, prompting her to burst into tears. Bencho beams with delight as she runs off, sobbing.

Iyer rings the doorbell, and is greeted by an ironed and starched Abhishek.

Accepting Abhishek's half-hearted obeisance – a vague swipe in the general direction of his feet – he takes off his sandals. From the main room, Abhishek's wife joins them at the door, holding a tumbler of coffee. She's pretty, if nervy-looking – the kind of woman who drinks her coffee in gulps.

'Uncle, my wife Lata.'

'Yes! You're Chandra's daughter, no?' Iyer asks.

'No, Uncle,' says the girl, bending to touch his feet, 'Seshan's daughter.'

They all look at Bencho, who is hopping on one leg, taking off his sandals and placing them in a neat row beside the other sandals. They easily qualify as the most ragged shoes in the row.

'This is Mr Bencho, soon to be a corporator,' Iyer says to Abhishek and Lata, stepping over the threshold.

'Mr Bencho,' says Abhishek, with an ugly emphasis on 'Mister'. 'Shall Mr Bencho do us the honour of eating at our table, Uncle, because we have a more suitable place for him to eat.'

Bencho looks down, wanting to be invisible instead of the fattest and most conspicuous person in the room.

'Abhishek!' Iyer says, sharply. 'Either he will eat with us or I will not eat at all.'

'But in our home the custom …' Abhishek starts, as Bencho starts putting his feet back into his sandals.

'Lalgudi's friend will eat with us, Abhishek,' says a voice from the top of the stairs. 'Please, Bencho, you are welcome.'

Iyer's brother, who is descending the staircase, is tall, clean-shaven and carries himself with great dignity. His forehead is marked with the Shaivite *tripundra*: the three parallel ash lines with a red dot marking the third eye. He is dressed in a better version of the outfit that Iyer wears: a well-cut black jacket over a spotless dhoti and white shirt.

'Lalgudi.'

'Arjun.'

The two brothers stare at each other. Bencho realises he has been holding his breath; that is the level of tension in the air. Then Arjun's wife comes down the stairs and touches Iyer's feet, giving him a warm smile.

'You look like a third-rate rowdy,' she says, smiling. 'You need a shave and haircut. And what happened to your forehead?' She comes closer to examine the bruise.

'That's my third eye – it opened' Iyer says, laughing.

Everyone laughs, more out of relief than amusement.

'I can smell the *sāmbhar*. Are we having *idlis*?'

'Yes, with fresh coconut chutney. The coconuts here come from Assam.'

The conversation is interrupted by the arrival of Arvind, Iyer's youngest nephew, who is dashing down the stairs towards him.

'Uncle!'

'Arvind! Hope you're failing at mathematics like I advised!'

Arvind laughs and Iyer gathers him into a bear hug.

'Ha, no Uncle, I got into IIT! All of them!'

'Excellent, you can become a mercenary like the rest of them,' Iyer says, asking for further details.

Bencho, who is standing there feeling out of place and awkward, is accosted by Arjun. 'Who are you?' Arjun asks in an undertone.

'I am a friend,' Bencho starts, almost losing the courage to complete the sentence. 'I work at the home in Kashi sometimes, sir. I was helping take care of Iyer Sir on his trip. He wanted to come home for Holi, sir.'

'You work at the home for the dying?'

'Yes, sir,' mumbles Bencho, not elaborating on his specific duties.

'Is he … better?' Arjun asks.

Bencho doesn't know how to answer.

'Come, wash your hands and let's have breakfast,' Vinita says, heading in the direction of the dining area, followed by Abhisek and Lata. They enter a small garden near the kitchen, where a table has been laid out under an awning.

'How is the factory, Abhishek?' Iyer asks as they settle themselves around the table.

'Better than before, Uncle.'

A servant appears, carrying a pailful of coconut chutney. He serves everyone, walking clockwise around the table.

'Delicious! Perfect!' Iyer cries, tasting the chutney. 'Try it, Bencho,' he says.

A cook serves a platter of golden *dosas* shaped in triangles in the traditional Tamil way, and Bencho examines everyone carefully before taking a bite, careful not to break any etiquette. The first *dosa* disappears. Iyer feels that he has eaten sunlight, the delicate fretwork of rice flour melting on contact with the functioning side of Iyer's mouth.

As the *dosas* become one with him, Iyer begins to recount his adventures, telling his family about rescuing the boy from the trucker named after – and surely sharing some qualities with – the evil emperor Aurangzeb.

Arvind and Bencho listen with rapt attention and Vinita giggles from time to time, but the rest focus on their food. Breakfast is nearly over when Iyer launches into the convict story.

'So the boat was full of prisoners, and instantly I knew I had to save these poor fellows. What fault of theirs was it, I thought. So I shouted out to the khaki monkey who—'

'Still the stories, eh, Uncle?' Abhishek pushes his plate away, smirking. His mother shoots him a warning glance, which he ignores.

'Stories?' Iyer asks.

'Yes,' he says, chuckling as if recalling a pleasant memory. 'Like when you'd give away your money, and my father's money too, because someone had spun a good yarn about how much they needed help. Like that old con man who tried to get you to sign the factory over to him. Remember?' he says, laughing.

'Abhishek,' warns his father from the head of the table. Abhishek looks tempted to continue but thinks better of it.

'We should leave, Bencho,' Iyer mutters, trying to stand but finding his knee somewhat stiff and non-cooperative from sitting down too long.

Arjun's wife looks at him, willing him to say something, but he looks down at his banana leaf, unable to rise.

Emboldened further by the lack of recrimination, Abhishek launches another salvo.

'How much money is this chap making off you, Uncle?' Abhishek says, indicating Bencho.

Iyer feels his palm clench into a fist when Arjun rises to his feet, shouting at Abhishek to leave the table.

Already embarrassed by his own outburst towards his fool uncle and his father's inevitable reprimand, Abhishek decides that obedience would only mean further humiliation. There is only one course to take, he thinks, which is to keep on going.

'We know what happened to you at the home, Uncle,' he says. 'We know they thought you were crazy, just like we did.'

'Take it easy,' Bencho says.

'Oh, you don't think he's crazy?' Abhishek says to Bencho. 'He's Bhīma, is it? He's a warrior? You believe that, is it?'

'He has travelled so far and has been so happy to see you. And he's a scholar, he has read and reread the holy texts for years. And yes, sir,' Bencho adds, feeling more courageous and looking Abhishek in the eye, 'I believe him, sir.'

'Ah, really. Did he tell you about his days when he owned a part of this company?'

'Enough, Abhishek, enough,' his father says, slamming his fist on the table. Abhishek bows his head, incapable of more disrespect, and silence reigns. It is so quiet that Iyer feels he can hear his tooth throbbing.

'Tell it, Abhishek,' he says, his shoulders drooping. 'Tell the story.'

Arjun turns away. Bencho shuffles. The awkwardless is heavy and low, bowing everyone's heads, shrinking their lungs, forcing them to hold their breath.

'My uncle here, who is so much better than everyone else, has treated me with nothing but contempt. He has created problems for me, for all of us, by managing to lose his birthright share in this company, by giving money away to thieves and con artists every day, and by bringing all sorts of unsavoury types,' – he stops and looks pointedly at Bencho – 'into our home.'

'He believes strongly in justice, sir, and compassion,' Bencho says.

'And alcohol,' Abhishek says.

Iyer doesn't move, but everyone else looks away. Bencho swallows a gasp.

'This "great *brahmachari*" was an obnoxious drunk. And my father had to cover for him.'

'Talk to me,' Iyer says. 'Not to him.'

'The truth is, he destroys everything he touches. And no matter what we tried to do, he did not stop. He *does* not stop. He *cannot* stop. We had to have him declared insane just to save ourselves, but here he is again. He turned out to be too crazy even for a home full of crazies.'

Iyer's lips tremble but he keeps sitting, a thousand-mile stare boring into the *sāmbhar*, which has turned into a miniature swamp with horned serpent-like entities swimming in its depths.

'You want the truth?' Abhishek asks. He has endured the breakfast by crafting a sentence that he is now longing to deliver. Abhishek delivers it with relish: 'He was an alcoholic asshole before. Now he's just an asshole.'

Iyer's forehead wound begins to weep, a little blood breaking the scab. It trickles into an eyebrow. He doesn't move to wipe it away. He looks like he's never going to move again.

Vinita reaches over and presses a handkerchief to Iyer's forehead. Iyer makes to rise from his seat, his toothache now throbbing loudly in his blood.

'He has never apologised. He has never said "sorry" even once to my father, who has dedicated his life to preventing us ending up in the gutter. Never! Not once has he had the decency to say "thank you",' continues Abhishek. 'The family knows I'm right, they just don't have the courage to agree to his face. Cowards.'

Arjun stares at his son across the table, but Abhishek does not look back, knowing that this would be the only time he would ever get the chance to speak his mind.

'How much are you making off him, Bencho?'

Iyer leaps across the table at Abhishek, knocking him backwards into his chair. With balletic control, his knees hit Abhishek's chest and knock his chair over backwards. As they fall, Iyer straddles his chest, pinning his arms down with his knees and grabbing his throat.

Arjun runs around the table, grabbing Iyer by the shoulders as everyone else looks on, horrified. Iyer is taut, unmovable. Abhishek's face has turned red as he struggles to breathe.

'Let him go, Lalgudi,' Arjun begs, shaking Iyer's shoulders as his son's face takes on a purple hue. Iyer sobs, releasing Abhishek and slumps down, exhausted. It's over as quickly as it had begun.

Standing over the gasping Abhishek and adjusting his coat, Iyer looks down at him, feeling a deep regret, a physical pain: a sorrow that rises from the earth and wraps around his heart.

'My dear boy …'

He reaches down to help Abhishek up, but Abhishek strikes his hand away, still trying to collect himself. Turning around, Iyer looks at the faces of his family: they look unsure, hurt, shocked.

'I am sorry,' he says, his chest contracting. 'Forgive me. For everything.'

Iyer reshapes his Brylcreemed hair with his fingers and walks towards the door. Lata and Vinita rush to Abhishek, helping him to his feet while Arvind sits openmouthed in his chair, not believing what has just happened. Bencho takes Iyer's arm and Iyer leans against him, pausing.

'I am living out my destiny,' says Iyer to his family. 'Forgive me for it.'

At the main entrance, Arjun places his hand on Iyer's shoulder, stopping him. He pulls Iyer into an embrace.

'Thank you … Bhīmaji,' he says.

Though no more words are exchanged, Iyer leaves feeling relieved and lighter. If he had looked back while walking away, he would have seen Arvind, Vinita and Arjun standing by the door, looking out after him and Bencho.

The Holi crowds that had been gathering in the morning are out in full force now. Bencho and Iyer walk past the effigy of Putna, her head a mud pot painted with fangs and eyes. The giant wheel has begun turning, and shrieking children fill its carriages. Iyer is oblivious to the chaos around him. He raises his hand to cup his throbbing jaw. Seeing this, Bencho excuses himself for a moment and sneaks off to the sweet-seller, who is ladling out sweetened milk from a large pot boiling on the side of the courtyard. Taking the remains of a ball of opium he'd saved in his pocket, he crumbles it into the milk.

'Here, sir,' Bencho offers, taking a glass himself and giving Iyer one. 'Drink it, sir. It'll soothe your tooth.'

As Iyer drains the glass, both he and Bencho get drenched from above. A gang of children burst out, hooting from a terrace before running away, cheering. Bencho and Iyer look at each other and Bencho smiles. Iyer grins too, the *bhang* beginning to take effect. Warmth flows through his limbs, replacing the aches with a feeling of gentle bliss.

More children rush towards them with coloured water and sprinkle them with dyes. Iyer notices an old man chuckling in delight, and is surprised to observe that it is himself.

A lightness takes over his body from the opium, and something else as well. Iyer shakes his head and smiles, recognising the something else as the feeling he had felt when Arjun had held him.

Gasping and wiping off the dye dripping from his face, Iyer feels that he has been awoken from the horror of wakefulness and taken into a pleasant, rainbow-coloured dream.

20

Shading his eyes, all Iyer can see are toothy faces looking down at him from the rooftops. A little boy darts around the corner and squirts him with a water gun.

'I am sorry!' shouts Iyer to no one in particular, and feels even lighter. A cackling old man pours a bucket of yellow dye on him from a rooftop; Iyer turns his head to receive the shower. Bencho, in the meantime, has spotted the sour-faced girl whom he had shoved earlier. She's a peculiar yellow colour now. Red and blue fairy lights on the giant wheel flash on and off, outlining the figure of a gyrating man with a soft drink in his hands.

A dance has begun by the Ferris wheel. A group of boys dance like Bollywood actors to a song playing on one of their cell phones, hips thrust forward and hands on their heads. Iyer watches them from under a peepal tree, its branches spreading out over a temple pond.

He sees one of them rubbing colour on a woman by the giant wheel, letting his hands stray towards her chest. He sees her cover her chest with her arms and walk away. He considers intervening, but his will to fight has been lessened considerably by the blissful fug enveloping his senses. Perhaps she doesn't need him. See, she's walked away and nothing untoward has happened. He looks at the man, who looks like he's trying to laugh it off to his friends. Then, egged on by them, he calls out to the woman. She doesn't turn back. He walks up to her and puts his hand on her shoulder as his friends hoot and cheer. He starts pulling her towards him.

Iyer feels like he is watching television – one of those scratchy newscasts shot on a cell phone – as he sees the men crowd the woman, one pulling off her scarf.

Iyer looks at the man's face, and as he watches, his head develops scales and his hair is sucked into his scalp, revealing a bumpy skull covered in scars and sores with two indents, as if horns have been broken off his head.

'I see you!' says Iyer, looking for his staff.

He sees other creatures in attendance, darker forms: a hunchback with three arms, a hairy Rakshasa with protruding fangs and scales on its face, and a thin, ape-like being with long arms that end in hooks, diseased and bent over.

'Bencho,' he cries, 'where is my staff?' Seeing a water-gun nearby, he grabs it instead.

Though his limbs feel loose, Iyer runs towards the boy now trying to feel the woman's breast and yanks him away from her, flinging him to the ground and placing a foot on his neck. Aiming the water-gun at him, Iyer pushes on the plunger, showering him with red dye. He watches him as his scales dissolve in the blast, leaving behind a gasping, stoned human.

One of his friends punches Iyer, knocking him down. A crowd surges forward, sensing entertainment, and Iyer watches their arms morph into tentacles, scales forming over their faces. An elbow hits his head and Iyer tastes blood. Someone grabs his legs and drags him through the mud. He struggles to keep his face out of the muck with his hands, walking backwards as it were, bruising his palms on the ground. They turn him over and start throwing dye and mud at him. Bencho runs to join him but is no match for the excited crowd, who hold him away from Iyer.

'Why have you forsaken me, dear gods?' Iyer says, looking at the distorted reflections of the crowd, blue tears flowing up his face, into his eyes and onto his forehead. 'You can take the masks off,' cries Iyer, and is punched as the mob twists and turns him in the muddy slush, cheering.

Horrific creatures of all shapes and sizes surround him. 'I see you. I see you,' he shouts, and above its minions, the monstrous form of the demoness Putna comes to life: the giant wheel revolving behind her, her gyrating figure alive with malevolence. The Ferris wheel begins to turn at this point; something is not oiled right. A screech rents the air – the sound of metal on metal. The fairy lights blink, outlining a figure that seems to be offering the crowds the soft drink he is holding, his hips thrusting wildly.

The mob surrounding him laughs, 'The old man hasn't had enough yet.'

The constable, who had been enjoying his Holi (for when there is too much to keep an eye on, you keep an eye on nothing) and had rather hoped to feel up a passing woman himself, sees the fracas and looks into it out of curiosity, wondering which drunk, drugged fool had got himself into trouble this time. He stands with the crowd, laughing, till he realises the mud-caked figure on the floor is Abhishek Sir's uncle. As he can't risk being pulverised by the crowd himself, he does the next best thing, which is to run off and return with help.

21

When Arvind and Abhishek arrive to fetch Iyer, he is out
cold, watched over by a distraught Bencho.

'He must have had too much *bhang*,' Abhishek says, lifting
him into the car and hoping he doesn't get too much mud on it.

'That crowd would have killed him,' Bencho says, annoyed at
Abhishek.

'It's only bruises. He needs rest, that's all,' Abhishek says,
looking away from Bencho, ashamed of his earlier outburst.

Arvind gives Bencho some money and tells him they'll take
Iyer back to the home in the car, and to get his boat fixed and to
go back in it himself. He thanks him sincerely for taking care of
his uncle.

Iyer sleeps through most of the journey from Allahabad to
Benares, his eyes swollen shut. Though his whole body aches,
Iyer feels strangely elated. Word of his exploits has travelled,
and there is quite a crowd at the home to receive him when he
reaches it. Even Mala cranes her neck out over the balcony to
watch, cursing him once or twice out of habit. As Iyer is helped
up the stairs to his room, Khanolkar seizes upon Abhishek, and

after offering unctous gratitude for Iyer's safe return, he asks a question to which he receives just the reply he wants.

Khanolkar purchases a long length of chain and a large Godrej lock, which he uses to chain Iyer by the ankle to his bed. The chain is just long enough for Iyer to reach the private toilet in the next room, though one leg stretches out horizontal to the floor when he squats.

When Dr Krishna visits, he questions the use of the chain but is told by Khanolkar that it is at the request of his family, and that it is for Iyer's own safety, and would Krishna want to be responsible for him escaping and getting himself killed rather than having some sort of restraint? On his next visit, Krishna brings a dentist who extracts Iyer's broken tooth, pulling it out with a pair of pliers after Iyer swallows several ibuprofen tablets. Visitors are banned, and Iyer is left to his healing and sedatives. He sleeps for most of the day, waking only eat, bathe, be medicated or receive long lectures from Khanolkar about the importance of dying in peace by the Ganges, steeped in faith and prayer, without which nirvana or a decent rebirth would be made impossible. He asks for Bencho but is told that he caught a virus on his return journey, and is also recuperating.

Khanolkar calls for a meeting with his residents with the objective of taking precautions to prevent Iyer from escaping again. 'This is the last time I want to deal with this madman going out and getting beaten up. Soon they will follow him here and beat me up.'

'He can open his eyes now, and most of his wounds are healing,' Krishna says.

'And the bastard is probably looking at the window to run off again,' says Khanolkar.

'He will bring ruin to all of us, for sure. Hundred per cent,' adds Mishra, sipping noisily.

'Sir, if I may …' asks Krishna, raising his hand.

'Who is capable of handling a madman such as him?' mutters Khanolkar, his voice growing shrill. 'I am at my wits' end.'

'If I may … sir!' asks Krishna, using the last traces of his midwestern American accent to gain attention, raising his hand again. Rising to his feet to gain control of the conversation, he addresses the gathering, 'Gentlemen, I think I know what to do.'

'Yes, what?' snaps Khanolkar.

'Where did he get that accent?' Mishra says sotto voce to Khanolkar. 'Duty-free?'

'All madness has influences, and our friend is a prolific reader. Is that not so?'

'Yes, he reads all kinds of books.'

'So first, we get rid of all his books. They've messed with his head.'

'I propose we burn his books. Or he will find some way of retrieving them.'

'Can't you just prescribe a pill to calm him down?' asks Khanolkar, not entirely comfortable with the idea of doing away with someone's possessions, as he may run the risk of being asked to pay for them at some later stage.

'A pill is insufficient, as we have learned. I believe that if we control what goes into Iyer's head, we can control what the rest of him does. We control his books, we control his head. And given the trouble he has created, a purge is required. Any questions?'

In the warmth of the afternoon, when many of the residents sleep, Krishna visits Iyer and contemplates his subject, who seems to sleep, covered in a white sheet, as if he is already dead.

His body is marked with wounds in various stages of healing. A few purple contusions radiating outwards from their centres like galaxies, a few cuts – some scabbed and others weeping, and deeper wounds that have turned into keloids, rising from his body like tiny fortifications on a battle-scarred landscape. The wound on his forehead has healed, and all that remains is its impression, shaped, thinks Krishna, like a flying crow.

Krishna whistles in amazement, deducing from the various stages of healing that there were very few gaps between injuries in Iyer's journey down the river.

'You know, the wound is the place where light enters you,' mutters Iyer, his eyes still closed.

'Or bacteria,' quips Krishna.

'You're still the same quack, Krishna?'

'Yes, sir. And it is Dr Krishna, not Krishna.'

'Dr Krishna, why am I chained?'

'They want you to heal your wounds and not run off,' Krishna says.

'Who will battle the advancing darkness, doctor?'

'I cannot see any advancing darkness, Iyer, and neither can you.'

'Yes, obviously, imbecile, because it is dark.'

'I studied psychology for a semester at Ohio State University. I might be able help you, Iyer.'

Iyer begins to laugh but it comes out like a wheeze, his eyes crinkling with mirth.

'You want to help me? America wants to help me? Everyone knows where that leads,' he says.

Krishna gives Iyer a thermometer, which he obediently pops into his mouth.

'How can a young man help an old man? He hash no egshperiensh of being an old man,' Iyer says, the thermometer under his tongue.

'Khanolkar thinks that you are clinically insane and has suggested you be moved to his cousin's mental hospital in Mirzapur,' says Krishna, taking the thermometer from Iyer's mouth and holding it up to the light. 'They keep the hard cases in rooms where they are attached to chains hanging off the walls.'

'A *brahmachari* swims in insanity. Modern men like you will drown.'

'Well, this *brahmachari* has a 102-degree temperature. You must rest,' says Krishna.

'I have sworn an oath to the gods that I will battle Bakasura.'

'What if he defeats you?'

'Then I shall have to be his slave for one incarnation. That is the heavenly rule.'

'Hold still, Iyer, I'm going to give you an injection now,' Krishna says, taking out the morphine and preparing the syringe.

'No, Dr Krishna. I do not wish to dull my pain. I approach my death. Can you not see?' cries Iyer, grabbing Krishna's arm with a surprisingly firm grip. 'I die soon. All your science cannot help it. We are powerless. Destiny fulfils herself no matter what you think.'

Unfazed, Krishna taps for a vein and gives him the shot. He waits for Iyer to sleep and then calls Khanolkar, who arrives with Mattroo and Mishra. They start dismantling Iyer's stacks of books and carry them out into the courtyard. By their third trip, there are no more books to take; only the *Reader's Digests* remain, warped and rotted after years of being soaked in phenyl every time the room is cleaned. Krishna agrees they can be left there, as they are unlikely to give anyone any ideas. Worried that Iyer would track his books down from any shop or recycling facility, Khanolkar douses them in petrol and sets fire to them in the courtyard.

Later that evening Iyer awakens, his head spinning from the morphine, and shouts for Khanolkar when he sees his empty shelves.

'Where are my books? Where *ARE* my books?' he sobs, shaking his chain about so hard that it rattles the bedpost.

Rushing up the stairs and into his room, Khanolkar tells Iyer that the Bakasura had come by and burnt his books, fire roaring out of his mouth.

'There is nothing but darkness in store if you burn the dreams of man,' Iyer shouts hysterically, trying to pull the chain off his foot. 'I have to stop him, help me.'

'We are helping you, Iyer,' Khanolkar says, trying to calm him down. 'It's too late.' He wonders if the book-burning has made things worse, but pushes the thought out of his mind.

'Come, come, Iyer, we all burn in the end,' Khanolkar says.

'It is not right to burn beings while they sleep. They will carry that agony with them into the next life. They will not know why they have been destroyed. "Who have *I* burnt to deserve this?" they will ask.'

'Come Iyer, they're only books. And you still have the *Reader's Digests.*'

'My books will reappear on some writer's pen someday. That is their magic. They will appear again.'

'They are ashes, Iyer, how will they appear again?'

'As a curse, Khanolkar. As a curse.'

As the days roll on, Krishna begins to gravely doubt his judgement. The wounds on Iyer's body are healing, but he refuses to speak, lying inert in one spot, barely wincing when his cuts are dressed, not making eye contact, let alone conversation. Krishna wonders if he should buy Iyer replacement books, but then feels that would be even more foolish. Nothing he has learned, in Ohio or in Kashi, has prepared him for such a patient.

The person who has healed in this period of time is Bencho. Drained after his journey, though his boat trip back had been relatively uneventful, Bencho has finally shaken off his fever with a long rest, and has drunk enough milk and turmeric to put some life back into his bones. He has dithered a great deal over visiting Iyer, since he hasn't brought him the best of luck in the past, but still, he has news for him. And he has something important to ask him – very important. He goes to the home and Khanolkar turns puce upon seeing him. He is banned from seeing Iyer and, indeed, banned from setting foot anywhere near the establishment. Given Khanolkar's rage, he is grateful just to have left intact. Still, he must see Iyer. Bencho has an idea.

Lying in bed, locked in his gloom, Iyer hears tapping.

'Sir!' Bencho hisses. 'Sir?'

Iyer doesn't answer, unsure as to whether he is imagining it, scared that he is now hearing voices, and also wondering why they are addressing him so formally.

'Sir, the window!'

Iyer turns and sees that familiar fat face, and is utterly disoriented. He stares at Bencho, bewildered.

'Go away, Bencho,' he says, 'I am chained. I cannot reach.'

'No problem,' says Bencho, forcing the window open from the outside and climbing in.

'It's good to be back, sir, isn't it?'

Iyer turns the other way.

'Sir, I need a favour.'

No reply.

'Sir?'

Bencho continues all the same.

'Sir, I've got the money to become a corporator; I'm going to go and meet MLA Jayachandra. Sir, I need you to come with me. You promised.'

'Bencho, I'm chained to my bed, I'm going to die here. I don't know what you're talking about. And where did you get that kind of money, anyway? Who have you robbed?'

Bencho looks down and says nothing.

'Think of it as a loan, sir. I will pay it back, but I need you to come with me.'

'A loan from who, Bencho?'

'A temple on the ghat. My cousin is the caretaker.'

'A temple?' Iyers says, sighing. 'You're stealing from a temple.'

'Not stealing, sir, borrowing. What is a few *lakhs* to the gods? And I will put it all back, and pay it off with honest service, sir. But now I need you to come with me to meet Jayachandra, sir, tomorrow. Meet me at Omnath's tonga at dawn.'

'I am chained here, Bencho, can you not see? Even if I wasn't sickened at you for stealing from a temple to bribe a corrupt man for the opportunity to grow corrupt yourself, I am chained to this bed and to my fate.'

'No you aren't, sir,' Bencho says grinning, pulling a key ring with one Godrej key out of his pocket. 'I stole the key from Khanolkar's office.' He tosses it to Iyer and climbs out of the window.

22

Just before the sun rises, Iyer undoes the lock, taking care not to rattle the chain, and changes into a clean *kurta* and dhoti. He does a few stretches to see what his body can handle and, satisfied, lowers himself down the side of the building to where Bencho waits, pulling on a *chillum* with Omnath under the cart. Trishala is loaded with supplies, and the three of them head towards the ghats.

This time, however, Krishna and Khanolkar are better prepared for this eventuality: they have told every policeman and every beggar in the vicinity about Iyer's proclivity for escape, and have set a reward for his information or capture. And so when Iyer is spotted by the leper he'd insulted during his last adventure, he calls Dr Krishna, who calls Khanolkar. They have only managed to get a few yards away when the two catch up with them.

'Where do you think you're going?' Khanolkar says, spotting Iyer and grabbing him.

Bencho shrinks away, casting around, looking for an out.

Krishna approaches him and says gently, 'Iyer, we're not trying to hurt you, but you might be suffering from mild dementia. Please let us help. Please, Iyer.'

'Let's all go back now, Iyer,' Khanolkar says in his most soothing voice. 'If you hate the chain, we'll take it off, OK? Let's all have a cup of tea, eh? Bencho can come too,' he says, smiling at Bencho with murder in his eyes. 'Why don't you come and join us for breakfast? We'll arrange something special.'

'I am not Iyer I AM BHĪMA,' he says as Khanolkar starts leading him back to the home.

Khanolkar stops when he hears the screech. An entire cavalcade, it seems, arrives, hurtling around the corner, barely missing Trishala and forcing Bencho to press himself against the betel-leaf stained walls. Bencho counts four SUVs with flashing red lights and a black BMW as they drive past him, sirens blaring, sending pedestrians and vendors leaping for cover. The cavalcade comes to a halt by the home. Looking over their shoulders, Khanolkar and Krishna see men in safari suits and policemen tumble out of the SUVs, roughly pushing back the crowd that has instantly formed around them.

A man gets out of the car at the front. It is the inspector whose dead father Bencho had dropped into the gutter. Bencho almost passes out from fear. Never mind his political career, he was unlikely to even live to see the afternoon.

'We are finished. I told you this would happen,' mutters a sweating Khanolkar to Krishna, smiling ingratiatingly as the inspector walks up to Iyer, *lathi* in hand.

Clearing his throat, the inspector addresses Khanolkar, 'I would like to speak with Mr Bhīma, *brahmachari*.' The police have finally arrived, courtesy of that lunatic, Khanolkar thinks bitterly.

'Yes, sir, of course, sir,' Khanolkar croaks, wondering what the hell Iyer has done this time, 'but may I ask what for?'

'My noble and precious queen asks for the honour of a word,' the inspector intones, as if by rote.

'Yes, of course! She may approach,' Iyer says, straightening himself.

'Open the door,' he says to a constable, motioning towards the BMW. The constable scurries forward and the door is opened. A blast of cold air and the odour of Eau d'Hadrien exit the vehicle. A manicured hand emerges from the shadows, followed by the rest of Ranjana in an immaculate white sari.

'We meet again, dear Bhīma,' she says with the same mischievous smile.

'My queen,' Iyer says, bowing his head.

'Let me introduce myself, again. I am MLA Jayachandra's wife. I wish to thank you for saving me from harm, and my husband wishes to thank you too.'

Krishna elbows Khanolkar in his ribs to tell him to shut his mouth, which has fallen open in an unseemly fashion. So has Bencho's, which now breaks into a grin. While Khanolkar tries to absorb the relief of the police not being here to drag him away to prison, Bencho pulls himself together, feeling that for once the fates are being kind to him, delivering to his doorstep the wife of the man he wanted to meet so badly. He bounces in front of Khanolkar, 'Maybe you do not remember me, madam, I am Bhīma's loyal companion. We are ready for any duties Mrs or Mr Jayachandra Sir may have for us. No problem,' he says, beaming.

'My queen, did you come to tempt this *brahmachari*, or are you bored with the company you keep?' Iyer asks, and Bencho wants to shake Iyer. He clears his throat meaningfully, but Iyer pays no heed to him.

'Great Bhīma, love brings me here. You inspired me to tell my husband about your great exploits that you dedicate to your true love. He wishes to see you with his own eyes, as he says no man as pure as you can exist.'

'Madam, if I may,' says Dr Krishna, stepping forward. 'With due respect, this man needs treatment. He is unwell.'

'I think I know the treatment Lord Bhīma needs,' Ranjana says, looking Krishna up and down. Krishna feels himself blushing for the first time in years.

'In truth, Bhīma, we need your presence for an important reason,' Ranjana says, lowering her voice as if revealing a confidence. Khanolkar, Krishna, Bencho and several dozen others lean forward.

'This is another game, isn't it?' Iyer asks, raising his chin petulantly.

'No game, sir. My dear husband, who is currently battling all kinds of dark forces while arranging the Kumbh Mela, is in need of your help and advice.'

'My help?' Iyer asks, surprised and instantly tempted.

'Yes. Absolutely.'

'What form has Bakasura taken to trouble your husband?'

'I will explain,' she says, 'as long as you promise to pledge your services to us. And hopefully my dear husband will spend less time arranging things and more time enjoying them.'

Bencho nods earnestly, 'Of course, madam, I give you my word.'

'So do you agree to come to our aid?' asks Ranjana, ignoring Bencho.

Iyer takes a deep breath, his eyes not leaving Ranjana's, and nods slightly.

Sighing with relief, Ranjana snaps her fingers for the car.

'Now come with us. You can sit with me in my car. Bencho can come in another car.'

'That will not be necessary, my queen. I prefer not to sit on dead cattle. I have my own vehicle,' announces Iyer, imperious again. 'And I always travel with Bencho.'

'Very well,' says Ranjana, turning to leave, anxious to get back to the air conditioning.

'What vehicle?' Bencho asks, wondering what he'd missed in the weeks he'd not spoken to Iyer. It seemed highly unlikely that that nephew of his had given him his SUV.

'Follow us then, Lord Bhīma. Let us not waste time,' Ranjana says, getting back into the car.

The inspector walks up to Bencho and says in a voice that could freeze mercury, 'Your cell-phone number.' Bencho stammers it to him and the inspector types it into his phone. 'Email,' barks the inspector, and Bencho stutters it out. He gives Bencho a missed call, and glares after them as Bencho and Iyer disappear into the crowd, Trishala in tow.

Krishna and Khanolkar look at each other in shock as the cars start pulling out of the square. Khanolkar is in a daze, and tries to approach the constables, but they ignore him, more concerned with clearing the road of cycle rickshaws.

'Where's Iyer?' whimpers Khanolkar just as the last SUV leaves the square and Trishala bursts out of a side street, attached to Omnath's tonga. Bencho is sitting in the driver's seat, Iyer standing erect on the floorboards next to him, one foot raised on the front seat, his hand extended and holding onto his staff, chin pointing at the horizon and the sun full on his face.

'Oh Iyer, no,' moans Krishna as the tonga rattles past, merging with numerous cycle rickshaws that materialise from nowhere.

'I'll bring him back, I swear,' Bencho shouts, cracking the reins as they disappear into the stream of traffic.

Khanolkar pauses in the middle of the road, his face blank, rickshaws whizzing about him. Krishna walks over and takes his arm.

'Don't worry, Khanolkar,' Krishna says, noticing his stupefaction. 'I have a plan.'

Damayanti is one of the people in the dispersing crowd. 'That must be the beautiful Panchakanya that mad bandicoot is in love with!' Mala says, wide-eyed, sniffing the air that still holds the scent of Eau d'Hadrien.

'Beautiful? She's a fat, disgusting pig!' Damayanti snaps, walking back home in a huff.

23

Trishala runs as fast she can but is outpaced by the cars, and is soon the only thing on a long and empty road. Seeing Iyer's mournful countenance, Bencho asks him what on earth has happened. He was so excited only a little while earlier, Bencho says.

'And now you can finally introduce me to Jayachandra!' he adds.

'My heart is full of sorrow, Bencho. I am confused.'

'What are you confused about?'

'About my duty, Bencho.'

'Your duty is to murder this Bakasura who only you can see, and also to persuade Jayachandra to give me a chance at a political career, remember?'

'Yes, Bencho. But murder, even of a foul demon, is a terrible thing.'

'Sir, don't worry. When I am prime minister, I will close the case.'

'I have no need of your favours Bencho, even if you were to become prime minister.'

'Then what is your problem?'

'What if this queen asks me to commit a crime? She has tricked me before.'

'Sir, just keep doing what you do and do not think of the end result. Before you know it, all will be over,' Bencho says cheerily.

'Really, Bencho?'

'Yes, sir. Really. Especially after you introduce me,' reminds Bencho, his smile fixed, an eyelid beginning to twitch.

'Really.'

'Yes. Really,' says Bencho, cracking the reins and giving Trishala a scare.

They ride along in silence. The terrain becomes hilly and Trishala slows down, Iyer getting off on inclines to make it easier for her. Cresting a small hill, they see that the cavalcade has stopped by a brightly painted circus truck parked by the side of the road. Its hood is raised, a small man hammering away at the engine block. The truck carries a cage partially covered with a tarpaulin. And within its bars, ignoring a cloud of flies, sits a massive Bengal tiger.

Trishala freezes, braying loudly, the smell of tiger rank in her nostrils. Jumping off the tonga, Iyer walks towards Ranjana, who is standing near the cage admiring the precious cargo.

'Aah, Mr Bhīma, come. All you men like to show your teeth when women are present, but why don't we see what happens with there are a few more teeth in the equation,' she says, smiling.

'This beast is caged, humiliated and tamed. The tigers I knew were fierce, wild and free,' Iyer says.

Iyer walks around the cage, the Bengal tiger's eyes following his every move.

'Do not come too close,' warns the man who had been working on the engine. 'He loves the taste of clowns.'

Iyer breathes in the smell of the tiger and closes his eyes. When he opens them, the tiger is not where it was; it glides towards the bars at a slight angle to Iyer, its tail twitching.

'My old friend. How are you? You must feel alone, caged and surrounded by monkeys,' says Iyer tenderly, a look of deep empathy on his face.

The tiger sits down, his orange eyes fixed on Iyer.

'We are alike, you and I. Don't you think?' he asks, and takes a step towards the cage.

Suddenly, without warning, Iyer knocks off the latch and the cage door screeches open.

There is a quiet, desperate rush for the cars, with much shoving involved. Trishala trots away hurriedly. In moments, Iyer is the only man standing in the open except for the keeper, who dashes under the truck.

Ranjana finds herself in the front seat, sitting on Bencho's lap, flanked by several bodyguards jammed into the car.

Oblivious to the chaos, Iyer continues.

'You and I see eye to eye. We understand each other but this modern lady does not.'

The tiger snarls, its face twisting, falling into a crouch. Ranjana gasps.

'You understand, don't you pussycat?' says Iyer unblinkingly. 'Do you want to stay in your cage and be chattered at by these monkeys? Or do you want one last great battle before I release you into a better birth from this inglorious time? I can do that for you, my dear friend,' offers Iyer.

The tiger yawns, its yellow canines half the length of Iyer's face, still crouched.

'We were free once. We were masters of our world,' intones Iyer, his eyes meeting the tiger's, who roars. Bencho cannot help but utter a suppressed shriek.

'Yes. I feel the same,' says Iyer to the tiger. 'I do not like talking. There is bliss in the world. Let us embrace it together, my friend. The way things were.'

Iyer steps back some paces and twirls his staff, ready for battle.

'I am ready. There are no cages where we shall go. Come, my friend, come,' Iyer says, speaking as though to a child.

The tiger crouches, its tail twitching and every muscle tensed, staring at Iyer, who stares back at him, twirling his staff. 'I am Bhīma, destroyer of evil, tamer of elephants and the master of the mace. I will free you.'

The keeper pops out from under the truck, whose length he has crawled beneath, and slams the cage door shut just as the tiger tenses to leap. The gates clang shut. Enclosed again, the feline circles the cage, snarling, its tail lashing from side to side.

'You are insane!' screams the keeper hoarsely, advancing towards Iyer with the spanner. 'He would have torn you to bits.'

'How dare you?' snaps Iyer, furious at being interrupted. 'I was teaching him how to be who he truly is!' Then Iyer pauses, and says thoughtfully to no one, 'Yet, his non-cooperation might also be a revolt against this modern age.'

Gasping with excitement, Ranjana tumbles out of the BMW, followed by the rest of her entourage.

'You *are* insane,' she says, running towards Iyer.

'All you brave men with machine guns! Come out of your hiding places. My sir, Bhīma, is not afraid,' laughs Bencho, directing his jibe at the inspector, but his laughter is replaced with a shriek as the tiger roars, swiping at the bars with his paw.

A strange feeling comes over Ranjana suddenly, a sense she hasn't had in a long time. Placing her hand over her ribcage, she *hears* her heart beat. She notices the risen hair on her arms and the clean, metallic taste of adrenaline. The air is cleaner, the scenery more pronounced now, and even single leaves are more defined and shine with colour. A spontaneous giggle leaps out of her mouth.

So this is being alive!

'Are you satisfied, my queen?'

'Not yet, Mr Iyer, not yet.'

'I am a little disappointed with that tiger. His spirit seems to have been caged for too long. I have known him in other avatars, when he would not have hesitated.'

'He still has his *animal* instincts, no?' says Ranjana, her lips parted.

'Animal instincts? A tiger in a cage only knows the cage. When we get used to our cages it becomes a habit. Keep that habit and it becomes your character. Maintain your character and in another life it turns up as instinct.'

They resume their journey. Ranjana's convoy speeds ahead, leaving the tonga straggling far behind. In the midst of endless fields dotted with stunted trees and bent-over farmers, the cavalcade reaches a large house with big gates, standing on acres of land and surrounded by rose gardens.

Ranjana's car enters the gates, stopping for her to instruct a gardener not to overwater a bed of sunset roses, shockingly orange against the black Gangetic soil. They drive past gleaming, velvety lawns, a pond, a crowd of waiting supplicants, and the security men leaning against their Maruti Gypsies, standing to attention but ignored, as Ranjana is driven into the car park at the rear end of the bungalow.

Preoccupied with tigers and fools, Ranjana enters the house, ignoring the barefooted farmers who crowd the entrance hall with repaired sandals attached to weathered feet and eyes that follow her across the room.

There is laughter coming from the office at the end of the corridor, and Ranjana bursts in, the guard stepping aside to let her pass.

Jayachandra sits at his desk, chatting with the commissioner. He's trim for his fifty-five years, dressed in a brilliant white shirt over grey slacks, looking happy and relaxed. A bottle of Laphroaig lies open on the sideboard; a sweating glass leaves condensation marks on the rosewood.

'I heard you found your fool?' Jayachandra asks, smiling. 'A genuine fool is very hard to find these days. What say, commissioner?'

'Well, as the fool would say, a fool thinks he's wise, but a wise man knows that he's a fool,' Ranjana replies.

'She has brought home snake charmers, travelling musicians, gypsies, and now this,' Jayachandra says indulgently to the commissioner. 'Our dear commissioner has reported to me that there is fear of a terrorist attack on the Kumbh Mela, different factions of Naga *babas* have been threatening each other over bathing timings, our local candidate has too many cases against him – the usual caste-violence nonsense – and the elections are just around the corner.'

'I can ask for help from Delhi. We can also try for a CRPF battalion,' the commissioner says, 'but I am not too sure about the Naga babas. They rush down to the water in thousands, so managing them could be difficult.'

'Yes, we also need to find a candidate from a lower caste – you know exactly which one, commissioner – to put up against our own candidate: not popular enough to appeal to our voters but good enough to eat into his opponent's vote bank. A proper man of the people, you know,' Jayachandra says, leaving his desk and exiting the room. 'We need to entertain them. Entertainment! An entertaining candidate for the elections! The Kumbh will look after itself like it always has.'

'Darling,' says Ranjana, 'I know just the man! Now, don't write him off just because … well, you'll see.'

Jayachandra nods at his capricious wife, intrigued as to what she is going to come up with this time. Hearing the tonga coming up the driveway, she stares out of the window and says, 'They've arrived!'

Ranjana had instructed the guards to show every courtesy to their new guests, and Bencho is most impressed when the massive wrought-iron gates are thrown open and a guard runs out into the road, blowing his whistle unnecessarily. They pass under unnecessary arches and into the rose garden, which is glistening from having just been watered.

Trishala, confronted with fields of moist petals after a long and tiring journey, decides to go her own way and walks into the rose beds, chomping at the blossoms. Bencho sees Ranjana on the balcony and waves, dropping a rein. His wave is unreturned and, feeling the slackness of her reins, Trishala walks deeper into the rose patch, chomping down on Ranjana's prized blooms, using her lips to delicately separate the blooms from their thorny stems. Bencho leans forward to retrieve the rein, slips off the cart and falls into a rose bush.

A hundred metres away, livid at seeing her prized blooms being masticated, Ranjana starts cursing vividly and Jayachandra bursts out laughing.

'My dear beautiful Ranjana, now I know why I love you more and more very day.'

'Damn them,' she says, her pupils pinpricks of annoyance, but Jayachandra places his hands on her shoulders and caresses them, making her close her eyes. She moans, ignoring the commissioner, who watches the scene with a lascivious smile.

'Sir, I knew with your influence I could get my corporator nomination,' says an emotional Bencho, pulling Trishala and the cart away from the roses, the wheels crushing several plants on their way out. 'What a big house! See, sir!' exclaims Bencho, adjusting his pants and pointing at a huge marble sculpture of Venus flanked by a statue of the goddess Kali amongst the roses. 'Look at how much we spend on the residence of just one politician.'

They reach the shaded front entrance and Iyer jumps off the donkey cart while Bencho unhitches Trishala. A wide series of steep steps lead to the oversized door. Bencho tethers Trishala and follows Iyer to the door. Behind them, a security man sits on a tin chair in the shadow of a bougainvillea. Bencho freezes when he sees him.

It is The Lover who glares at them from his folding chair, a sten gun on his lap.

'You, sir,' Iyer says, inclining his head in The Lover's direction graciously as Bencho gasps with fright.

The Lover stares at Iyer, unslings his weapon and rises to his feet.

24

He walks towards and past them, Bencho flinching as he passes. He pushes open the door and stands there, looking bored.

The Lover's face is blank except for his scar, which pulses like a living creature.

The door opens into a massive hall. The Lover announces their arrival.

'Brahmachari Bhīma and …'

'Bencho,' hisses Bencho, looking into the dimly lit hall and not seeing anything except for a few underweight labourers crouched over tables.

'Bencho,' intones The Lover, staring into the middle distance, his voice echoing back at them from the shadows. The hall extends fifty metres into the shadows, and the eastern portion of the room opens into a wide verandah that overlooks a secluded bathing ghat where the river roars by at great speed. Further downstream, visible through the windows, is Prayag, the confluence of the Ganges, Yamuna and Saraswati. Flocks of gulls are whirling above the meeting point, their distant screeching audible through the barred windows of the room.

Steel racks fill the halls in rows that recede into the darkness. Rows of outdated computer terminals stretch along the far end, covered in dust and plastic sheets, the remnants of botched and forgotten government schemes. The ground is littered with rat droppings, and they can hear bats in the asbestos roof forty feet above. Some of the racks contain old files and various government records, while others have been cleared and are filled with antiquities, mainly bits and pieces of temple carvings, heads, hands and torsos that are lying about on shelves and in piles on the floor.

A large, dreaming Vishnu occupies a table, covered in bubble wrap, its face destroyed. Gandhara Buddhas are being wrapped in gunnysack cloth and plastic packing on another table, blissful heads sticking out of the bubble wrap. A damaged Durga seated on a legless stone lion is swaddled in cloth and plastic, its sword emerging like a flagstaff. Further to their right is a table with a pot of tea and a bowl of fried cashew nuts, laid out like an offering at the foot of a massive six-foot-high Nataraja – an avatar of Lord Shiva, the Lord of the cosmic Dance – one of his four arms pointed delicately towards his left foot, poised over the little demon Apasmara Purusha, the embodiment of ignorance, whom the Nataraja crushes with his right foot, matted locks whirling about him as he dances endlessly within a circular arch of flames, the endless cycle of birth and death, creation and destruction. It is the only undamaged sculpture in the room.

Iyer is transfixed.

Om Namah Shivaya.

He is overwhelmed with the beauty of the unmarked sculpture.

'Hello!' says Bencho, feeling apprehensive, his voice echoing in the hall. 'Where are these things going?' he whispers to Iyer.

'It is an honor to have the great *brahmachari* Bhīma in my humble abode. And his faithful friend as well.'

Before Iyer can answer, Jayachandra himself is seen walking down an aisle from the other end of the room towards them, accompanied by Ranjana and a group of people: the commissioner, The Lover, the inspector and Jayachandra's secretary, a flamboyant-looking man with a thin moustache in a Charagh Din shirt. Jayachandra's face breaks into a smile as he sees Iyer and Bencho.

'Take a deep breath. You can smell history in this room.'

'Good day, dear queen and king,' says Iyer, bowing theatrically as they approach.

'And a good day to you too, sirs.' Bencho moves behind Iyer, feeling unbearably nervous at being addressed by the MLA.

'Is something bothering you, Bencho? Is there anything I can do for you?' Ranjana asks.

'If you don't mind, madam, there is,' Bencho says, looking out from behind Iyer. 'My donkey has not eaten today. She needs some grass and a shady spot, please.'

'Go and feed the donkey,' Ranjana says to the inspector.

'And do not approach her from the backside or she will kick you. Like this,' Bencho says, bending over and kicking backwards. 'Approach her from the front and grab her like this,' he says, turning to the man next to him and demonstrating, realising too late that it's The Lover.

'Bencho!' Iyer says under his breath, and Bencho quickly releases him.

'If she tries to kick you, kick her back! Or she will lose respect for you and kick you the next chance she gets. Understand?' says Bencho earnestly.

Jayachandra laughs out loud, delighted with Bencho's intricate request, noting the amusement on the faces of those present. The Lover's scar is now so red, it looks like a fresh wound.

'Fighting demons must be tiring work, *brahmachari*. Why do you do what you do?' Jayachandra asks, walking up to the dreaming Vishnu and motioning for Iyer to approach.

'One feels happiness when on the true path. And with the gods as company too.'

Jayachandra laughs at his double-entendre.

'These gods are the ones I've saved, not the types that save us,' Jayachandra says, touching the Vishnu.

Iyer moves to the Durga statue – a deity he has often invoked as protection against the night – now covered in packing material, her eyes fierce even when cast in stone, staring out from the midst of straw and Thermocol.

'What is so fascinating about Hindu goddesses is how they can be so many forms,' Jayachandra says, looking at Ranjana. 'She can be Durga, Parvati or Kali. She can be dark or fair, violent or peaceful, angry or blissful. She can be a loving mother, a terrifying killer or a transcendent lover. She can be married or single, a man-eater or a lover. She can cradle you in her arms or tear your heart from your chest.'

The confidence with which he holds forth, Bencho notes, is like Iyer's confidence, only that Jayachandra's is based on his power here on earth.

'To answer the question you're undoubtedly asking, the gods are paying for the living. I try to ensure progress, Bhīmaji. See these lands, on which farmers are toiling under the sun. I want to make them like Bangalore or Delhi one day. What do you think of that?'

'I have visited both Delhi and Bangalore a few times: concentrations of sweatshops and malls, apartments without water supply and false promises from billboards. These cities reveal a great civilisation in decline.'

'That's better than slaving away in a field, no? Beset by snakes and insects? I am working very hard on a book now about the pursuit of progress. I believe that we live in an intelligent time and we are fortunate to be born in this modern age.'

'Many believe that all a man needs for the acquisition of truth is to use his brains, and to work hard. The ascetic life is frowned upon, but the *brahmachari* knows the connection between the knowledge of truth and his own purity. The intellectual life is but an expression of the moral life. Only he who keeps the vessel clean will receive the truth, and *kripa* is necessary for this.'

'*Kripa?*'

'The Christians call it grace.'

'Ah yes, grace. Yes,' Jayachandra nods.

'We experience the world with our senses and speak of it with words. But our souls are structured differently, which is why we feel that something is always missing, that some aspect of us lives outside words, beyond what can be thought.'

'Well, one's truth is as we make it. It is separate from what we do. Many of our modern thinkers had lives filled with sinister dealings and illicit relationships, but their conclusions were profound, both in terms of effect and logic. Would you agree?' Jayachandra asks.

'One must conform desire to the truth and not the other way around, my king. One must be the truth to let it flow through you. Otherwise what flows through you is contaminated, and one would be destined to be reborn a cockroach, or worse.'

'You are afraid of change, my friend,' says Jayachandra. 'You live in fear of the new. My duty is to ensure *progress,* my dear Bhīma. Spiritual satisfaction is not my problem. My job is to give them what they *want* – factories, movie theatres, malls, restaurants and cars. Come, progress is not be feared, my friend. It can make life easier.'

'I do not wish for an easy life, sir, I wish for a good life.'

'Tell me *brahmachari*, may I ask you a personal question?' Jayachandra says, beginning to tire of the conversation.

'Yes.'

'Who is this woman Punchi ... Pancha ...?'

'Her name is Panchakanya, of Kashi.'

'Panchakanya? I sent my people to Kashi but there is no Panchakanya at the ghats. Inspector Sharma has checked.'

'She has been bewitched, like much of the world today. Only I know her true self, and that is more divine than anything you can imagine.'

'I remember the days when I was like you. I am honoured to have you as my guests. Show them to their rooms!' Jayachandra says.

The duo turn to depart, escorted by various helpers who materialise from the entrance.

'One minute,' Jayachandra says as they are led away. 'Bencho, is there something I can do for you?' catching Bencho unawares as he fills his face with cashew nuts from a bowl on the table.

'I want the chance to join politics,' Bencho says, his mouth full. He doesn't risk waiting to swallow them first, recognising that this is his time. 'Without paying ten *lakhs*,' he adds, trying to swallow and not choke to death. 'Sir, I have the whole of Benares in my hand. People know me, they trust me, I am one of them. Ask anyone who Bencho is, they will tell you.'

Jayachandra looks him up and down, smiles at Ranjana and turns to The Lover, 'Show Mr Bencho his town tomorrow morning to begin campaigning for the upcoming elections. I think you're just what we're looking for, Bencho.'

Bencho freezes, cashew nuts falling from his mouth and fists in equal numbers.

'Sir? Sir? Are you allowing me into your party?' Bencho says incredulously, spraying nuts with every word.

'No, I am not. You will run as an independent in a rival party's constituency. Let's see how you do. Iyer will stay here in the meantime.'

'Thank you, king,' says Iyer, bowing. 'Thank you, queen,' he says, bowing to Ranjana. 'Thank you all!' Bencho says, bowing to the room. 'I will do his utmost, my UTMOST! I only want what's best for my city, for all you, my people ...'

'Thank you, Bencho,' Jayachandra says, cutting his speech off. 'I will help you with the funds. The worst that will happen is that you will eat into my candidate's competitor's vote bank. Let's try you out. OK?'

'Sir. Thank you,' Bencho says, his eyes filling with tears as he bends to touch Jayachandra's feet. Cashew nuts fall from his pockets, scattering all over the floor.

'Get up, Bencho, this isn't necessary.'

Bencho bursts into tears and falls to his knees, grabbing at both Iyer's and Jayachandra's legs. Jayachandra steps back and out of reach, wondering if Bencho's hands would leave marks on his trousers, while Iyer steps forward and places his hand on Bencho's head.

'See, Bencho, I told you,' says Iyer, a tender smile on his face. 'The world is yours.'

'Jaya *hai*, Jaya *hai*, Jaya *haiii*,' sings Jayachandra under his breath, mimicking the national anthem.

They are led from the room, Iyer feeling happy for Bencho, and Bencho still sniffling with joy, tears streaming down his face.

The Lover smiles, too.

25

The preparations for the Kumbh Mela are in full swing. Krishna sits in the guts of a disembowelled truck, lost in thought. For some reason, he's been reminiscing about his time in America a great deal more than usual, recently – from the frozen streets of Columbus to the filthy ones of Kashi, from big silences to a constant soundtrack. Finished with his education. Finished with his brief stint at the clinic. Just like that. All those walks with snow crunching under his feet and the sound of tyres on asphalt – so far away now. The Olentangy River flowing under the frozen surface, dead squirrels and branches pressing up against the ice. Like it never happened.

He had fervently hoped never to be the Indian who went abroad and then struggled with his return, and he hadn't been one until now. Perhaps this was not dissatisfaction, but a sloughing off of a past life. Still, all these details played on his mind – how tyres on the road sounded different in America. The welcome back home, where skinny taxi drivers at the airport were clawing for his baggage, insisting he take their taxis. His new sneakers dirty within minutes of arriving, a fleck of *paan* on his sleeve like a welcoming *teeka*. He had enjoyed the peace of the clinic, the pace of life here, the slow vanquishing of the sort of control he had had over his life in the States. He didn't have control over much here, and he had found it relaxing. He had felt more connected to people here, where everyone was more at each other's mercy. Still, his mind threw up images of great big oaks changing colour in the fall, and of neat houses filled with large, white people.

The truck's organs are spread out over the floor in pools of grease. Salim, his hands blackened from a lifetime of working on the insides of a truck, squats on his haunches, a dented welder's mask covering a greasy face and a blowtorch licking at a part of the fuel tank, held in place with his bare feet. Around him lies a suit of armour made up from various pieces of the truck.

'Krishna, this is the first time I have been asked to chop up truck parts to make a costume. Why couldn't you just have something stitched? I don't understand.'

Krishna lifts a freshly made black helmet and tries it on. It fits.

'Well, they don't make truck parts like they used to,' Salim says, his blowtorch cutting through a section as if it was butter.

'Make sure the suit can withstand a beating, that's all,' Krishna says, his voice muffled from within the helmet.

'I thought this was for a drama production!' Salim says.

'Every day is drama for the theatre enthusiast!'

Krishna is distracted at the sight of a group of urchins arguing at the entrance of the scrapyard.

'Get lost!' Salim shouts, waving a jack at them.

'A new leader has arrived!' shouts one of the urchins, running towards a commotion further up the road.

'A donkey has arrived,' shrieks a second child, running in circles like a helicopter.

Curious, Krishna leaves the scrapyard and walks down the road towards the sounds of chanting and a village brass band belting out 'Auld Lang Syne' to a Bollywood beat. He is alarmed when an unmistakable name filters through the chatter, 'Bencho, Bencho, Bencho!'

Breaking into a run, Krishna pushes his way through the crowd and bursts onto the main road, gasping out loud when he sees what everyone else is looking at.

Trishala, decorated with garlands arounds her neck, is leading a motley procession, brought up in the rear by a scruffy and energetic brass band. A grinning Bencho sits on the donkey, wearing a monkey cap that leaves only his eyes and nose visible, a flowing red cape dragging on the street behind him. A procession of paid beggar *sadhus* recruited from Kashi by Jayachandra's party walks alongside Bencho, while behind them walks The Lover accompanied by several of his flunkies.

'I have come, dear people. I have come to save you,' Bencho bellows as benignly as one can bellow, waving to the crowd, his way cleared by the flunkies. Behind the brass band, two monkey trainers hold aloft a banner of Bencho's party symbol – a donkey.

'He's on a donkey. He does not even have a car!' shouts someone, and the crowd roars with laughter.

'If I travel at high speed, I will be removed from you people! It's good to be in close proximity to you, no?' Bencho says.

'Who speaks? The donkey or Mr Bencho?' The voice is coming from a long-haired *sadhu* wearing a chastity belt, his dreadlocks touching his calves. The crowd roars with laughter.

'When the leader sits on a donkey, it is very funny. But when a donkey sits in the leader's seat, it's no joke,' Bencho shouts back, the crowd roaring its approval at the quick retort.

'For more than sixty years you have not got the joke. I am happy you get it now,' shouts Bencho, goading Trishala forward as the band strikes up a marching tune.

A passing pilgrim garlands Trishala, and the crowd loves it. They start chanting, 'Bencho, Bencho, Bencho,' once again. Trishala has sufficient sense of occasion to behave for once, and walks in a straight line.

A large woman rushes into the street, dragging with her a trembling, dishevelled man wearing the uniform of a postal clerk. His shirt is torn, and he's holding broken spectacles.

Raising his arm, Bencho signals the brass band to stop and the procession halts.

'What is the matter, madam?' he asks, motioning for the crowd to fall silent.

'Sir! Sir! I have been paying this fellow bribes for my dead soldier husband's pension for fifteen years now, and he has increased his rate today.'

'Sir,' says the clerk pitifully, shaking his head in protest.

'Is this true?' asks Bencho, glaring at the clerk.

'Beat him!' someone yells.

'Hang him!' shouts an urchin, and the crowd roars its approval again, a few boys running forward to manhandle the clerk.

'Hold on! Hold on!' Bencho says, raising his hand authoratively and getting off the donkey.

The boys withdraw, disappointed, and the crowd falls silent.

'Pickpocket, you are forcing a widow to pay up half her pension. True?'

The man is silent.

'Is it true?' Bencho shouts, sticking his face very close to the trembling clerk's nose.

'Sir, yes, sir,' he sobs.

'You're the worst kind of parasite, targeting a poor widow.'

Some of the mob run towards the clerk and grab him again.

'Hold it! Keep calm everyone, keep calm,' shouts Bencho, which they do, looking just as confused as the clerk. Turning with a flourish, he walks towards the woman much like lawyers in courtroom scenes in movies do, his arms clasped behind his back.

'And you, madam. You said that he has been doing this for fifteen years? True?' he asks, stopping abruptly.

'Yes, sir.'

'Then, madam,' barks Bencho, helping himself to some peanuts from a cart, 'why is it a problem now?' Crushing a peanut and extracting the kernel.

'He wants more money now, sir, almost double.'

'Almost double? It's *how much* you are paying that bothers you, not paying the bribe. True?' asks Bencho, helping himself to a peanut from the peanut vendor's cart.

'Sir?' she asks.

'There is an ancient saying: if you give the monkey one peanut every day, one day he will want two.'

Seeing the clerk smile at this, Bencho kicks him in his rear to an approving cry from the crowd.

'Bencho Sir is a corruption fighter,' screams a voice, and the chant resumes, this time with renewed energy. '*Bencho Bencho Bencho.*'

Bencho takes the widow's arm and pushes her hard, sending her flying into a cloud of dust. The crowd falls silent as she rolls forward and bumps into a goat, the chanting petering out.

'And you, madam, should not feed monkeys,' he shouts, peanuts falling from his mouth.

The crowd is silent, all except the long-haired *sadhu* wearing the chastity belt, who claps and roars with laughter. Bencho takes another handful of peanuts from the cart as the woman rises to her feet and runs away, cursing.

'Sir, five rupees,' says the peanut vendor.

Bencho searches his pockets, his mouth full. He has nothing. He looks through his shirt pockets, then his back pockets, then his socks. The crowd leans forward, expecting a climax.

The Lover steps forward and pays the man with a ten-rupee note.

'Jayachandra Sir said to take care of all expenses.'

'Really?' says Bencho, and grabs another handful of peanuts before mounting Trishala.

'Peanuts for everyone,' he shouts and throws the handfuls of nuts into the sky. The crowd surges forward, singing Bencho's praises and grabbing peanuts from the cart as The Lover tries to stop them, his arms spread.

'Guavas for all,' Bencho shouts by another vendor's cart, and the mob rushes forward again, The Lover getting shoved in the bargain. 'Come along,' Bencho says to The Lover, 'you're going to have to learn to do this quicker if you're going to work for me!'

With guavas in their mouths and peanuts in their pockets, the crowd surges forward, raising slogans and praising Bencho. Bencho is led on his donkey towards the marketplace, a street child at the reins.

'Bencho Zindabad!' goes up the cry as he makes his procession through the town, vendors rushing forward with their produce, word of his generosity having already travelled around the marketplace, Bencho helping himself, leaving The Lover to fight his way through the crush to pay the bill.

'Bencho Zindabad!'

The day passes in a whirlwind, with Bencho touring the town and listening to various grievances and ideas, and finally meeting with a corporator to discuss schemes for the improvement of the town. Bencho's ideas for manhole preservation go well with the corporator – an honest man who is impressed with him and thinks of him as practical, a man in touch with reality and with a sound knowledge of management.

Evening descends, and Bencho is filled with a deep sense of civic duty and happiness. He also notices a new attribute in himself that he feels has eluded him for long – courage.

The Lover has been instructed to install Bencho in the guest quarters, a separate building on the Jayachandra estate, and he does so somewhat reluctantly. The rooms are opulent, the staff subservient, the bed massive with a noisy wall clock over it. Bencho examines the toilet, washing his hands in the health faucet, squatting on the European commode Indian-style, and using a Bisleri water bottle for his ablutions. He saves the plastic bottles of shampoo and conditioner to take home, and wraps the expensive Dove soap back up in its paper covering after using it. He smells like a spring meadow, Bencho thinks to himself, his senses singing.

He makes a cup of tea using an electric kettle for the first time, switching it on and off and on again to see what will happen. Hearing a car pull in, he walks to the window. He sees a truck arrive and then he sees the driver. Is it, could it be…? It's Aurangzeb, whom Iyer had beaten up earlier! Jayachandra himself has stepped out to speak to him, and The Lover has appeared too. His truck is being loaded with enormous gunny bags. They are the same ones the idols were kept in, which Bencho had seen earlier in the hall. A Durga slips out of her bag and is quickly wrapped up again.

Taking his new cell phone out, Bencho records a video, making sure to get Jayachandra speaking to the driver and The Lover. He doesn't know why, or what he's going to do with it; it's just an instinct. Bencho crawls into the huge bed, the sound of the wall clock loud and ominous above him. He sinks into the mattress, and after tossing and turning for a while, gets off the bed.

'Sir?' he says, for no reason, as Iyer is not there to speak to.

Bencho takes a blanket and pillow off the bed and, spreading the blanket on the ground, lies down on it. It has been an incredible day, but everything seems out of place. The clock seems to grow louder, and Bencho crawls under the four-poster bed, taking his bedding with him – the room a bit too large, the ceiling a bit too high and the bed a bit too soft for comfort.

26

As Bencho sleeps, Iyer is otherwise transported. He had been escorted to his room, a large affair with marble floors and velvet curtains, where he slept into the evening, tossing and turning, beset with auguries, the house of his childhood reappearing, the pool in the garden filled with wounded gods bleeding onto the lily pads.

In the early hours Iyer awakens to a knock, and an inexplicable feeling of soul sickness grips him from within.

A flunkey invites him to have tea with Ranjana and Jayachandra.

'Bencho, where are you?' mutters Iyer as he rummages through his backpack looking for his comb. He finds it and combs his hair, wincing when it drags over a wound. Dressed, he meets them on the verandah, overlooking millions of pilgrims, their settlements stretched for miles, the air humming with their prayers.

'Ah, Iyer welcome' says Jayachandra and pulls out chair for him. A pot of tea is served.

'Your man, I hear, did a decent job yesterday. I am waiting for a report on his progress. Who knows, your servant might get a few thousand votes.'

'He is not my servant.'

'Really, but he's a Dom isn't he? My sources say hes a con man, a drinker and fool,' laughs Jayachandra.

'He is much more than that,' says Iyer, suddenly angry, pushing the table away and rising to his feet.

'Don't feel bad, Mr Iyer. That was just a joke. Come and have a biscuit,' says Ranjana.

'He is ... he is ... my friend. And he is far more capable than you think,' retorts Iyer

'Really, that idiot? Capable of winning?' giggles Ranjana, unable to resist.

'He is no idiot! The only idiots I see are right here,' snaps Iyer.

'Relax. Have your tea. Lighten up,' Jayachandra says, motioning to a bearer who brings in a tray of food.

'You insult my friend. You mock his abilities and you use him,' Iyer snaps, and walks away, ignoring Jayachandra, who calls him to stay, and almost colliding with The Lover, who enters the verandah.

'It was all in fun. Entertainment!' shouts Ranjana.

'Degenerate entertainment fills the void when the divine has been replaced. Your entertainment reveals the pathetic nature of discourse in this age.'

'Ya, whatever, go to hell, then,' says Ranjana, furious, and Iyer walks off to his room, where he packs.

'Bloody moron! How is the other idiot doing?' asks Jayachandra.

'Sir, the whole town wants him back tomorrow,' says The Lover.

'What?'

'He is a great hit, sir. He will definitely win, if he stands,' says The Lover, a tiny smile playing at the corners of his mouth

'What? Say that again?'

'Sir, the people like him. He solved a dispute today! I mean, they *really* love him,' says The Lover, enunciating his words.

Jayachandra stares at The Lover and motions him to another room.

When Iyer wakes, he goes for a walk down to the banks of the river. On the opposite bank, the tented city stretches out beyond the horizon. He exhales and inhales purposefully: inhaling the air, exhaling his hurt. It is inconceivable that he had succeeded in getting so far, that he had managed to remain alive, and that he had not disappeared yet. The opposite bank thrums with life; the Kumbh, numberless thousands, hundreds of thousands, have come to bathe at the confluence at this auspicious time. Officials and lifeguard boats patrol the chaos as thousands of gulls circle above, mindless of the prayers below.

Iyer walks towards the river and undresses by its edge, folding his clothes and placing them on a rock. He can see the *sadhus* milling about on the other bank, dusting themselves with holy ash and draping marigolds over their bodies, preparing for their sacred bath.

Dressed only in a loincloth, Iyer walks into the shallows and looks down at the water by his feet. A school of tiny fish dart around his feet as they sink into the mud. When Iyer stops thinking, he is taken by wonder at the world of plants, fish, water and silence. It fills him like a vibration travelling through the marrow of his bones. Tingling with it, he steps into the brown water, wading to where the water is waist-deep and immersing himself in the river, chanting between immersions:

Om Namashivaya Namaha
Om Namashivaya Namaha
Om Namashivaya Namaha.

Iyer loses himself in meditation, staying beneath the surface for as long as he can, the sense of being underwater a balm, the little fish around him a miracle.

When Iyer rises for the third time, he hears a scream. It's not just any scream, it's a familiar sound; he's heard it many times before. He's often been the reason behind it. It's Bencho.

27

On the peach satin bedspread, Bencho is holding up his arms to fend off blows to his most painful places. The Lover and another goon are on top of him, punching and pulling.

'You are impersonating a government servant. The penalty for that is severe,' the goon says.

'What ...' Bencho gasps, in shock.

'How much have you raised for your campaign? Where is my share?' The Lover says, kicking him in the ribs.

'I have not taken any money, sir! You paid everyone. You had the money!' he says, 'I didn't have any. I didn't take any.'

'Liar! Robber.'

The goon drags him down the corridor, taking care to kick and slap him at every opportunity, past a large bronze Nataraja that seems to turn its head to look. Bencho breaks away and runs a little way down, but they catch up with him and hit him again for trying to run away. The sounds of drums and chanting echo over the water and into the house. The Kumbh Mela is in full swing, tents lining the banks and sadhus blowing on conches, singing their praises to Lord Shiva. *Om Nama Shivaya* booms over the water, the vibrations resonating in their chests.

'No, please,' Bencho cries as he's dragged out onto the sand, his nose bleeding, and pitched over the embankment wall. Rolling down the slope, he comes to a stop near Trishala, who has been tied to a tree by the river.

The Lover slides down the embankment after him and starts again. Bencho is no match for him, and focuses only on avoiding serious harm by protecting his head and groin as far as he can.

Sobbing, Bencho tries to escape by crawling into the water, but The Lover follows him. The flunkey joins in and wades into the river too, tearing Bencho's shirt, jamming his face into the slush so that his mouth fills with mud. When their arms tire, they use their feet on him.

'Why are you doing this?' Bencho asks, feeling as if he's going to pass out.

'You owe me an apology for your rudeness, but for now, my dear, I'll be content with just one eye. You can choose which one.'

Bencho screams, but is held firmly in place by the goon.

'Which one?' The Lover grins and moves the tip of the blade of his dagger from eyeball to eyeball, breaking the skin under one eye and then the next, making it look as if Bencho is crying tears of blood.

'Which testicle shall I smash, and which one shall you keep?' comes a voice from the top of the embankment. Iyer, freshly bathed and naked but for a loincloth, stands there holding his staff.

'Come closer, I cannot hear you,' The Lover says, smiling. The goon moves towards him, but The Lover stops him and releases Bencho, who promptly collapses.

'I see you,' Iyer says, seeing scales growing over The Lover's face.

'Come, old man. Let's see who *you* are, my dear.'

While he speaks, Iyer sees his skin turn grey, and spikes rise from his skin like a swamp-creature loaded with venom.

Iyer steps off the embankment wall. A shining iron shield lies in the sand and Iyer picks it up, fitting it to his arm. The Lover watches, bemused, watching Iyer slip his arm through the handle of a broken plastic bucket. Iyer twirls his staff and feels the earth beneath his feet, the sand between his toes. He inhales fresh air, feeling it enter his lungs. From the corner of his eye, he sees Bencho stumbling to safety.

The Lover feints with the knife and rushes forward, holding the blade close to his torso while swinging away with his other arm. Iyer waits at the top of the slope and parries the blade away with his staff. He swings back at The Lover, who falls to his knees, allowing the staff to pass over his head while slashing at Iyer, who leaps out of the way. Simultaneously, he uses the staff like a battering ram, smashing it into The Lover's face and knocking him off his feet as he slides down the embankment.

Bencho, moving with difficulty, has taken Trishala a short distance up the slope, where he slaps her on the rump, sending her away for the time being. Breathing deeply, he tries to calm down a little, trying to stop himself shaking. He sees another man join them on the ghat; they are more flunkies of Jayachandra's, and Bencho knows there is an endless supply of them. They are not attacking Iyer yet, merely standing around him. The Lover is on the ground, dazed by Iyer's attack.

'Hit him, sir, hit him,' shouts Bencho, half turning to flee, but Iyer waits for The Lover to recover before striking again.

'HIT HIM!' Bencho shouts.

The Lover rises, smiling, spitting out a tooth. He looks for his knife and finds it shining in the black sand. Crouching like an animal, he rushes forward, grabbing a handful of sand at the last second and throwing it at Iyer's eyes. Stabbing wildly, The Lover connects with the bucket, the blade going through it and getting stuck. Iyer rips the knife away and is himself pushed down into the sand.

Wiping the sand from his eyes, Iyer is back in his earthly avatar. The scales have disappeared; The Lover is human. Iyer tries to rise but cannot, dazed by the scuffle. Bencho turns tail and runs.

We live in a weak light. But darkness was here before. And it will come again.

The Lover grabs Iyer around the neck in a headlock and brings the knife to his throat, the blade cold against his skin.

28

Iyer feels the skin on his neck stinging. There is no pain. He feels vaguely disconnected from his predicament, as if there is a goat being slaughtered elsewhere. Slowly, The Lover exerts more pressure, teasing the blade over his skin, his lips parted, savouring the moment. The sun shining in his eyes awakens Iyer, and he feels the beginnings of shock. A shadow falls over the scene. Bencho seems to fly overhead. *How can this be?* Iyer wonders.

Your true form.

Bencho lands atop The Lover with his full weight, having leapt off the embankment, smashing him into the sand. Bencho kicks him on the jaw for good measure. The flunkies advance. Bencho knocks one on the jaw with Iyer's staff, and the other backs off.

Gasping, spitting out sand, The Lover raises himself onto his hands and looks for his dagger, as Iyer tries to reach his staff. He finds his dagger just as Iyer swings the staff into The Lover's crotch with all his strength. It connects, with the sound of an axe hitting wood, and The Lover crumples into a foetal position on the sand.

A conch blows.

They hear the Naga *sadhus* prepare to charge the river at the exact auspicious time, ten thousand of them chanting the name of God.

'*Om Namashivaya Namaha*,' roars the crowd, making the hairs on Iyer's arm stand up.

The Lover tries to move, his face contorted, but falls back down again. The conch blows again, and the *sadhus* roll over the embankment, waving banners and swords, resplendent in marigolds and armed with *trishuls*.

Om Namashivaya Namaha.

Iyer and Bencho begin to run. They run to the end of the private ghat and climb over the wall into the common area, amongst the immense crowd beyond the walls. Immediately overwhelmed by the size of it, carried like flotsam by its momentum, they are separated. Iyer is forced into the confluence, which is shallow for hundreds of yards, all the way to the centre.

Long-haired and almost naked, Iyer is indistinguishable from the ecstatic bathing *sadhus* that surround him, praying and chanting. He limps through the crowds chanting the names of the gods.

Feeling faint, he sits in the water as the faithful immerse themselves, eyes closed, mantras on their lips, water dripping off their beards. An old ascetic is helped into the water, and hobbles to a spot next to Iyer. He immerses himself, helped by a younger *sadhu*, and then bursts into tears for reasons he cannot understand. He prays and gives thanks and prays again, the river wrapping around his waist.

Again and again I seek comfort from you.

'*Om Namashivaya Namaha*,' he says, grateful tears streaming down his face.

Iyer lowers himself further into the coolness and immerses himself, hearing nothing but the sounds of the river. He touches the earth beneath the water with his hands and lowers his forehead to the riverbed, holding his breath as his head goes beneath the surface, letting his skull sink into the black soil, brought down from the tops of mountains that were once the bottom of the sea.

29

The suit of armour is securely packed in its cardboard box. Krishna had planned to meet Iyer at Jayachandra's house later that day, before making the return journey, hopefully with Iyer in tow, if his plan went well. But when he'd tried Bencho in the morning, all he got was his devotional ringtone till it cut out without an answer.

The Tempo Traveller takes ten hours to reach Allahabad from Varanasi. Khanolkar had made it wait for two days to make the journey profitable, and half the neighbourhood had piled into it, paying Khanolkar enough to recover the fare twice over. The driver, a thin boy with yellow eyes and brown teeth, was to drive the Tempo all the way to the Kumbh Mela.

Bags are loaded onto the roof of the Tempo and tied down. Everything is delayed by Mala, who climbs in at the last minute without paying Khanolkar. When he tries to remove her, she says she will put such a frightful curse on him that he will regret this moment for the rest of his life. Something in her eyes makes Khanolkar override his lack of generosity; he lets her in and even gets Damayanti to accompany her, in case Mala hurts herself and curses Khanolkar anyway. When the overloaded Tempo eventually starts moving, Khanolkar takes the pillion seat, berating the driver for going over speed breakers too fast and lecturing the pilgrims on the importance of the day and his contribution to their journey.

'Makar Sankranti marks the arrival of spring, and it is also regarded as the time for new beginnings and new endeavours. It marks the end of the inauspicious phase, which begins around mid-December. Mala Madam, stop putting your head out of the window – a bus will take it off. Put it back in. OK fine, leave it out. We will not even stop to collect it if it goes.' Krishna plugs in his earphones and listens to music on his phone.

Delayed by checkpoints searching for terrorists, they reach Allahabad at seven in the morning. The Tempo stops close to the river, near the innumerable tents stretched out on the dry bits of the riverbed. Come the monsoon, all this would be under water, the refuse of millions removed by a single season.

The little group pours out of the Tempo, stretching and unfolding their limbs after the cramped journey, then stands still for a few minutes, awed by the spectacle. Khanolkar takes this opportunity to read from his cell phone in a schoolteacher's voice, '"Kumbh Mela is a mass Hindu pilgrimage of faith in which Hindus gather to bathe in the sacred Ganges. It is considered to be the largest peaceful gathering in the world, where between sixty to a hundred million people visit the river. It is held every third year at one of the four places by rotation."'

Ignoring him, the group gathers their belongings close – sixty million attendees also means a good few thieves – and treks towards the water, negotiating the crowds, Krishna's cardboard box is conspicuously bulkier than everyone else's bundles of clothes and tiffins.

'"The name Kumbh Mela comes from the Hindi 'Kumbha', meaning 'a pitcher', and 'Mela', meaning 'fair' in Sanskrit. The pilgrimage is held for about one and a half months at each of these four places, where it is believed that drops of nectar fell from the

Kumbh carried by gods after the sea was churned,"' Khanolkar says, though no one can hear a thing now.

The auspicious side to bathe on is across the river, and Khanolkar haggles over a boat, settling on an exorbitant price. The demented Mala seizes control of the bow.

"'Bathing in these rivers is thought to cleanse one of all sins. This is where Brahma, the Creator of this Universe, attended a sacrificial ritual ...'"

Wrapped against the cold, they make their journey across the Ganges towards the other bank, even Khanolkar struck silent by the throbbing intensity of the chanting coming across the water in waves. Krishna feels as if he's near tears, but doesn't know why. They head towards the spotlights on the bank, silent and bathed in yellow light, awed by the atmosphere.

The quay is being manned by security guards holding Sten guns, helping people on and off boats and shouting at anyone being disorderly. Together they bathe, leaving Mala and Khanolkar to mind the bags. Holding hands, they immerse themselves, offering up prayers and doing the necessary rituals with little oil lamps and flowers. After bathing, they retreat towards the walls of the Allahabad fort, which plunges into the river on one side. There they change and open tiffins to eat while the sun dries their wet clothes. Krishna has brought his good camera with him, because this is too amazing to just use his phone's camera. He wants to post it all on Facebook later, and hopes his American friends will see how astonishing it is.

A very old man and his wife walk towards the river cautiously, supported by knobbed bamboo canes, their belongings in a gunnysack carried by the man over his shoulders, though not without difficulty. They walk so slowly that it seems they'll never reach it. But they keep going through the crowds, stopping and standing perfectly still whenever a ruckus breaks out near them, and then carrying on again. Krishna takes a picture of them, and of a man dunking a screaming child into the water. There are so many pictures to take that his finger is beginning to hurt from clicking the shutter, and he hasn't even started on the ascetics yet. He trains the camera on a group of *sadhus* further down the river, when he thinks he sees a familiar figure.

30

Iyer still feels dazed, his ears ringing with prayers as a group of *sadhus* surround him. The memory and adrenaline of his fight with The Lover are still so fresh on his mind that even the dazzling sky seems too much to absorb. A narrow jetty stretches for hundreds of metres, from the bank to where the rivers meet. The authorities have released just enough water from the dam to allow for safe bathing; the centre is waist-deep. The shallow, fast-flowing Ganges meets the deep-green Yamuna and somewhere in the middle, the invisible Saraswati flows into them.

I will swim in the Saraswati.

Making it to the centre, he looks around for Bencho, who can't be seen in the multitude. He feels a frisson of anxiety, wondering how he is going to make it back to Kashi; he can hardly go back to Jayachandra's and ask for a lift now. Still, these are small things, he thinks, in the grander scheme of things. A way will come to him.

Iyer sits down in the water with only his head protruding from it. He leans backwards and floats on his back, his hair floating loose about his head like a halo. Some bathers mistake him for a Himalayan *rishi* and throw marigolds at him, one woman telling her friends, 'He has floated for his whole life,' with great confidence. Conversations filter across to him, and he makes out snippets about real estate and the cost of food as thousands of brown-headed gulls wheel and circle above.

One old man, in a sea of beings, unworried about the cost of living.

Iyer laughs.

It would be so easy to sink down into the alluvium, so easy to disappear, to unite with the river, and that, too, at such an auspicious time.

And no one would miss him except maybe Bencho.

A gull shits on his forehead, interrupting the reverie, and Iyer sits up, scrubbing the excrement off furiously. Cupping water in his hands, he splashes it over his face, and over his neck and chest too, just in case.

'Sir,' he hears, 'sir, sir.' It is Bencho, making his way towards him in the water. 'Sir, I have found you.' Reaching Iyer, he bursts noisily into tears, his whole body still jangling with pain from his earlier beating, and – the shock of that subsiding – the end of his promising political career.

'Look at the bright side, Bencho, the worst has happened, now it must only get better,' Iyer says, gently.

'Sir, I have lost everything. Everything!' Bencho heaves as he sobs, dipping his head into the water to clear away his tears, and then weeping again.

'No, Bencho, we have won everything. We have broken free from the world's temptations. We have triumphed over all of Bakasura's evil designs and remained pure, no matter what has come our way.'

'I will never become Crucho, sir. That man, he would have killed me. You told me someone would write about us one day? What story will he have? That we got beaten up all the time? That is no story, sir. That is no *plot*,' he says.

'You have triumphed. We have everything, Bencho, everything is right here,' exclaims Iyer, taking a handful of water and letting it fall through his fingers. 'Our *integrity* is our offering. Our *existence* is our story! The journey lies within us, Bencho, and we are already victorious.'

'I have everything?' Bencho asks, trying to follow. He looks around as if there might be a clue somewhere, when another flock of brown-headed gulls passes overhead, shitting this time on Bencho's shoulder. Bencho doesn't even move.

'Bencho! We shall get you another town. Don't worry,' Iyer says, gently wiping his shoulder clean with water. 'You shall get another town, and I will defeat Bakasura,' Iyer says.

'What if there is no demon, sir?' Bencho says, hanging his head miserably. 'What if there is just this?'

Iyer doesn't comment, but starts to wade towards the bank, Bencho following silently.

'Sir, what more do you need to do? I want to return to Kashi.'

As they reach the bank they both think they hear something, but ignore it amidst the din and scrum of worshippers.

'Bhīmaaa!'

This time Bencho and Iyer look up towards the sound.

An ape-like creature of sorts stands above them on the bank. It is dressed in armour, carries a plastic baseball bat and wears a helmet with spikes rising up from it. Beneath the helmet, long acrylic hair flows. Gunnysack cloth makes a smock under the armour. The creature leaps off the embankment and lands in the water, drenching them. It leaps to its feet, twirls the plastic baseball bat and moves forward like a predator.

'Bhīma! I have travelled across time and space to destroy you. Prepare to die.'

'Who are you?' Iyer asks, pushing Bencho behind him and moving forward, his eyes flashing. 'How dare you challenge Bhīma of Kashi?'

'I am Bakasura, Bhīma! And I will challenge whoever the hell I want to. And now, you are most certainly going to die,' the demon says theatrically, in a rather familiar voice.

31

'Oh, shut up,' Bencho says, seeing through the disguise in an instant. 'We nearly got killed earlier today and now you want to fool around like this? Idiot!'

Iyer pushes Bencho aside and glares at Bakasura, swaying.

'*Rakshasa*! Prepare to die!' Iyer says, and points his staff at the masked Krishna.

'Sir, please stop. It's just the doctor,' Bencho says, as Krishna attempts a demon roar that sounds more like a dog howling, hammering the water with the plastic baseball bat.

'Bencho, tell Panchakanya of this exploit, no matter what happens.'

'If I defeat you, you must give up your pursuit of me. Understand? That is the ancient rule, as you know. If I defeat you here, now, it is over, Bhīma!'

'He agrees. He agrees!' Bencho says, comprehension dawning. 'I will tell Panchakanya whatever you want.'

Iyer shouts and charges at Bakasura, his staff held ahead of him. Dodging him, Krishna kicks water into Iyer's face and lunges forward, whacking him across the shoulders with the bat, which bends in half.

Krishna twists the bat back into shape, keeping the sun behind himself and in Iyer's eyes.

'HA! Foul beast, your paltry weapon falls off my heavenly muscles,' Iyer says, swinging his staff at Krishna, who ducks just in time. The staff continues on its trajectory, its momentum causing Iyer to lose his balance and tumble into the water.

Standing over him, Krishna laughs, 'So much for your heavenly muscles! Concede, Bhīma!'

'Never!' shouts Iyer and kicks at Krishna's crotch, missing and connecting with the breastplate. Howling in pain, Iyer grabs his foot and Krishna jerks the staff away, twirling it around and placing its tip on Iyer's chest, forcing him backwards so that he falls into the water.

'Do you concede defeat? That is the heavenly rule!' Krishna shouts, pressing down on the staff.

'The heavens can go to hell,' Iyer says through his pain, as Krishna presses down harder on the staff, forcing Iyer underwater. Dropping the staff, Krishna jumps onto Iyer's chest and forces his head under. Pulling Iyer's spluttering head out of the water, Krishna barks into his face.

'Will you accept that I have won?'

Iyer spits a stream of water into the visor covering Bakasura's face.

'Never. I will never surrender,' he splutters.

Cursing, Krishna shoves him under again and holds him there.

'He will never agree,' Bencho says, placing his hand on Krishna's shoulder. 'Enough.'

Krishna raises Iyer's head from the riverbed and Iyer spits again, but with less force than last time.

'Enough,' Bencho says, grabbing Krishna's shoulder, but he slaps it away and holds Iyer down again, pulling him up only when the bubbles pouring out of Iyer's mouth start dying down.

'Do you concede, Bhīma?'

Iyer chokes and tries to spit but the water dribbles out the side of his mouth.

'Concede, sir, please concede,' Bencho says from over Krishna's shoulder.

'I cannot,' Iyer gasps and punches the helmet, his hand rolled into a fist.

'Agree or die, Bhīma,' Krishna says, frustrated beyond words. He was so sure his plan would work. Not just was it a waste, but he's all out of ideas now, and God only knows what it'll do to their relationship if Iyer sees he's been attacked by his doctor.

'Finish it,' Iyer says, seeing Krishna remove his helmet. He peers at him, recognition dawning along with disbelief. 'You too, Dr Krishna, you too?'

Wearily, Krishna lets go of Iyer.

'Please agree,' a familiar voice says, and Iyer turns towards it. Damayanti stands freshly bathed and ethereal on the embankment, the late-morning sun rising behind her.

'Please agree, Iyer Sir, Panchakanya will be happier if you are alive.'

Iyer looks at her, then at the gulls wheeling above him, and finlly turns to Krishna. 'It is over,' he says, shoulders slumping. Krishna helps him up to his feet, one arm around his shoulders.

Trying to stand on his own, Iyer finds he cannot; his knee has locked up again and a sharp pain radiates through it. He tries to bend it, but it remains as stiff as a bamboo staff.

32

The Lover's back pain is bordering on unbearable. After he limped to the bank after the fight, he found an upturned boat and sat down on it. Getting up is proving hard; he clenches his teeth and raises himself inch by inch. Walking to a teashop, The Lover leans against a pillar.

His phone rings. He grimaces at the vibration and tries to fish around for it in his pocket without too much movement, though the action of reaching for the phone unleashes a nasty twinge up his back. When he finally gets his hands on the ringing phone, he sees it's not even his. Come to think of it, that sound isn't even his ringtone. He's about to scroll down the call log when he has a better idea. Opening the photo gallery, The Lover finds endless selfies of Bencho: Bencho on his donkey, conducting his campaign. Bencho lying on the vast bed in the guestroom, smiling. Bencho's photograph in the gilt-lined mirror in the bathroom. Bencho's head peering out from the shower curtain. What an ass, The Lover thinks, not for the first time. He's about to exit the gallery when he sees a video. He clicks play. It's Jayachandra. In front of him is the truck into which the idols are being loaded.

At least one is visible. There's even a shot of the consulate address that they're being dispatched to. I must say, Bencho, The Lover thinks, not such an ass after all.

He goes to settings and finds that the video has also been saved to Bencho's cloud storage account. Taking his own phone, The Lover calls Jayachandra and shares his surprise at Bencho's entrepreneurship with him. They both have the same idea of how to deal with him.

33

Inspector Narasimha Sharma doesn't answer his phone, standing in the quay near where his mother is bathing. He's not looking at his mother, who's almost done with a long ritual that guarantees the delivery of her prayers to his deceased father. The inspector is watching Iyer and Bencho who, along with the other day-trippers from the home, are sitting on the bank surrounded by everyone's drying clothes. Iyer is speaking and everyone is listening. The inspector can hear the sentence, 'I will not do what the darkness says.'

Helping his mother out of the water, Sharma helps her as she lights a *diya* with shivering fingers and releases it into the river. They return to the bank, where she joins the rest of the family. Satisfied with her comfort, Sharma walks over to Bencho and taps him on the shoulder.

Bencho is startled, and automatically raises his arm as if to ward off a blow.

'I don't want to hit you, Bencho – relax! But I just got a message from our friend Jayachandra. They found your phone and the video.'

Bencho goes pale and automatically starts scrabbling around in his pants for his phone, knowing that what he said was true.

'They want your cloud password,' Sharma says, enjoying Bencho's terror.

'What do I do?'

'Give it to them and leave now, before they find you,' he says.

'I don't remember it myself!' Bencho has gone white and appears to be having trouble breathing.

Sharma's phone rings again. He takes the call and interjects with 'yes sir's.

'Who was that?'

'That, Bencho, was my commissioner. You should leave Allahabad, or there will be consequences. Sometimes people are arrested for all sorts of things, things they may not even have done … you know how it goes.'

Bencho nods, knowing only too well.

'I am going to the bridge checkpoint by boat,' the inspector says. 'If you leave the city, come that way.'

Krishna has changed into clean trousers and a fresh shirt, and Iyer is back in his Mysore suit. Dry and dressed, the group has collected by a tea stall.

Seeing Khanolkar, Bencho sidles up to him and begs him in an urgent whisper to prepare for the journey back home.

'Sir, please. We must leave and not waste a second. It is a matter of life and death.'

Despite never having been his biggest fan, Khanolkar nods at the sight of Bencho's grey face. The relief of seeing Khanolkar showing him some compassion makes Bencho break down. He quickly explains the last two days to him, everything – the promise of being made a politician, how The Lover had tried, and very nearly succeeded, in murdering him, and also the bit about Jayachandra's illegal antiquities trade and the little video he had made of it, and of the statues in their cases. Khanolkar does not interrupt and listens, whistling in amazement at the more astonishing moments.

Without delay, Khanolkar rounds the group up, running after Mala, who can always sense when she's required to do something and does the opposite. In this case, she had taken off towards the water again. He marches everyone towards the boats in a single file, not even haggling, Iyer with his stiff leg being helped by Bencho and Krishna. They cross the river, huddled against the wind, Iyer falling asleep by the time they reach the other bank.

They pile into the Tempo, Khanolkar and Krishna shouting for the driver, who stumbles towards the vehicle, his eyes more yellow than usual. Bencho carries Iyer on his shoulders; his exhaustion has properly caught up with him and he hasn't stirred since he got onto the boat. The luggage is tied onto the rack and Krishna helps the driver, an expert luggage-catcher, by throwing the bags up at him. With everything secured, the driver takes over the wheel, getting berated for drinking by Khanolkar, who sits next to him, anxious for the journey to begin. Old yellow-eyes reverses onto the road, hitting the accelerator a bit too hard, and the rear end of the Tempo touches a passing truck's fender, ripping off its own rear bumper.

Both vehicles brake and Khanolkar curses, hitting the driver on the back of his head with his palm.

Bencho jumps out of the passenger seat onto the road and screams, wagging his finger at the truck driver, who also jumps out.

'You son of a whore, watch how you drive!' Bencho shouts.

'Yes, you son of a whore, watch how you drive,' adds Khanolkar, his long neck sticking out of the front window.

When the driver Aurangzeb and Bencho recognise each other, they are equally astounded.

The passenger door of the truck opens and The Lover jumps out, wincing in pain as he lands.

'You again,' he says to Bencho, his pupils constricting to pinpricks. Not wasting a moment, Bencho turns tail and runs towards the Tempo for his life. Shouting for the driver to start, he jumps in and clangs the door shut just as The Lover reaches it. He tries to yank the door open, hammering it with his fist and screaming in rage, hitting his own head on the window in an attempt to break the glass. Mala starts to cry, and Damayanti strokes her hair and makes soothing sounds. Krishna glances at Iyer, who hasn't stirred.

Taking a step back, The Lover picks up a fist-sized rock.

'Leave now,' Bencho shouts at the top of his voice, but the driver is having trouble with the gears. The stone shatters the side window and Khanolkar wastes no time, wrenching the driver out of his seat and taking the wheel, methodically tapping on the accelerator, easing the gear into place and starting the engine as another stone smashes through the window, hitting him on the shoulder.

'Hurry, sir,' Bencho says, whispering, The Lover smashing at the remnants of the window with another stone. He puts his hand into the vehicle, searching for the door handle as Bencho struggles to hold it closed. The Tempo starts, and the door is yanked open just as Khanolkar reverses. Holding on to the door, The Lover is carried along, lifted off his feet. Swerving left, Khanolkar executes a perfect turn onto the road, flinging The Lover off the road and into the mud, and narrowly missing a group of priests, who scatter, their begging pots clattering across the road. Revving the engine, Khanolkar yanks the gearstick into second gear and takes off properly.

Waking, Iyer throws off the blankets swaddling him and hobbles to the rear window in time to see The Lover as he runs back towards the truck, screaming at Aurangzeb to start the vehicle. Hitting the accelerator, Khanolkar comes to a bend in the road and, watching from the rear window, Iyer loses sight of the truck. Just as he sits back and exhales, it bursts out around the bend again, barreling towards them, smashing a guava vendor's cart.

'To arms! To arms!' shouts Iyer 'Where is my staff?'

'No, sir. It's on the roof, sir, and don't leave your seat,' Bencho says from the driver's cubicle as Khanolkar swerves around a camel caravan, throwing Mala off her seat and into the aisle. Shrieking, she climbs back up and holds on for dear life.

Bencho, hanging out of the shattered front window, yells at people to clear the road, waving a rag as the senior citizens sit there in quiet terror, years of living experience having taught them that screaming is a waste of energy.

Ignoring Bencho, Iyer moves to the last window, holding onto the seats to keep his balance as the Tempo hits maximum speed on the potholed road. The only way to the roof and his staff would be out of the window closest to the ladder that runs up the side of the Tempo. Mala occupies the last seat, holding on to the grille with both hands, her feet wrapped around the armrest in an effort to not be flung off again. 'Get away from me, demon,' she shrieks.

'Mala Madam, please let me get to the window. I have to save us from these *dacoits*,' Iyer says, eyes wide in supplication. 'Please, madam. Please.' Iyer claps his hands together.

Still holding on with all limbs, Mala begins to curse, but finally relents as Iyer keeps begging. She shuffles out of her seat and Iyer quickly opens the window, reaches out and grabs the external ladder. Pulling himself out, he climbs out of the Tempo and onto the ladder, holding on with great effort, using his stiff leg for support as he sits on the window, his legs on the inside. Carefully, he grabs onto the ladder and inches his way out of the hurtling vehicle. He sees a truck coming towards them from the opposite direction, and using all his strength, reaches the luggage carrier in the nick of time, barely avoiding being knocked off the bus.

I will overcome.

'Iyer is on the roof,' Mishra says, suddenly noticing the activity. Bencho turns to look just as Iyer's feet leave the interior of the bus.

Iyer crawls down the roof of the moving Tempo towards his staff, reaches it and wrests it free from under the bags. Holding it tight he

sits up, facing the truck that follows them and getting clobbered by
the green twigs of a low-hanging tamarind branch. Dazed, he leans
forward with the impact, which stings more than it stuns. He turns
his head to the front and is hit again, this time by the hanging roots
of a banyan tree. Iyer falls back on the bags, dazed.

The clouds seem not to move, still and immense overhead.

I am flying.

The truck has gained on them, and even though Khanolkar
has floored the accelerator, the Tempo does not go beyond eighty
kilometres an hour. As Khanolkar pulls on the choke, willing the
Tempo to go faster, the truck slams its rear bumper. Khanolkar is
hurled forward in his seat with the impact.

'Please, sir, I cannot do this,' Aurangzeb says as he bashes into
the Tempo again, the revolver pressed firmly to his ribs.

'Oh yes, you can,' The Lover says, hitting Aurangzeb across
the face with the revolver and jamming it into his ribs again,
twisting it hard to inflict maximum pain.

'Take them off the road, bastard,' The Lover says. Aurangzeb
touches the truck's accelerator, but lightly this time. Noticing the
deceleration, The Lover jams the revolver into Aurangzeb's neck,
grabbing his hair with his other hand.

'Hit them, or I will kill you and *I* will drive.'

Aurangzeb believes him.

His face hardening, Khanolkar presses down on the accelerator,
the choke on full, pushing the Tempo, which rattles like an auto-
rickshaw as Aurangzeb hits the rear bumper again, forcing the
Tempo to careen across and off the road into a field. Struggling
with the wheel, Khanolkar just about manages to right the vehicle
and speeds back onto the road in an explosion of dust.

Bencho reaches the window but is too corpulent to get through
it. He cries for Iyer to return, but the sound is lost on the road.

The road has narrowed, and drops off on its right side via a
steep incline into the deep river that flows along, thirty feet below
the speeding vehicles.

'We've got them,' The Lover says as the truck gains on the Tempo, the road ahead of them clear.

On the roof of the Tempo, Iyer recovers his senses and sits up, this time keeping an eye out for branches. He manages to bend his knee a little, and yanks out a bag tied to the luggage carrier. He flings it at the truck speeding not more than fifteen feet behind them. The bag explodes on the bonnet, sending dhotis and underwear flying onto the windscreen.

'Hit him again,' The Lover says, seeing Iyer on the roof, and Aurangzeb accelerates, almost touching the Tempo. The Lover raises the revolver towards Iyer, but Aurangzeb slows down, so he points it at Aurangzeb instead.

The next bag is heavy and contains Krishna's armour. Iyer pushes it off the Tempo and onto the truck's windscreen. It shatters the glass, the armour cascading into the driver's cubicle. Blinded by the rush of wind and a breastplate that jams the wheel, Aurangzeb brakes, the truck threatening to go off the road and hurtle down towards the river. Aurangzeb jams the brakes with all his strength, both feet pressing down, and manages to stop the truck a few inches from the edge of the drop. Dazed, he pushes the bullet tank off the bonnet, his hand going through the shattered windscreen.

'I am Bhīma!' comes the cry, half lost to the wind as the Tempo groans away into the distance. The Tempo's passengers break into a cheer, and Krishna leans over and pats a grim-faced Khanolkar on a back wet with sweat. Khanolkar is rigid with tension and does not speak. The engine splutters and the exhaust belches out black smoke. The fuel-tank line has been damaged, and the pointer on the gauge drops. They are leaking diesel.

A kilometre ahead, a police barricade has been set up in front of a bridge that stretches into a mist descended over the Ganges. Inspector Sharma is visible, standing in front of the barricade that has. Waving, he flags them down. Seeing the inspector, Khanolkar brakes, stopping the Tempo in a massive cloud of dust right in front of a petrol tanker waiting to have its papers checked. Ignoring the curses of the tanker driver, Khanolkar jumps out of the Tempo and into a herd of cows. Straight-backed and grim, he strides towards the inspector, slapping cows out of the way, ready to make his complaint.

'Inspector!' Khanolkar says, as steadily as he can speak, 'I have a complaint to make.'

Meanwhile, Bencho exits the Tempo and rushes to the external ladder, scuttling up it to help Iyer off the roof.

'Sir, you did it, you chased them off.'

'Bencho, my leg hurts,' Iyer says, exhausted.

34

Spitting bits of broken glass out of a bleeding mouth, The Lover orders Aurangzeb to get the vehicle back on the road. He does so, albeit at a slower pace, and they proceed, wind whipping through the windscreen. The Lover puts on Aurangzeb's sunglasses and wipes his face clean with his sleeve. In a few minutes they see the barricade in the distance, the parked Tempo, the cows and Khanolkar slapping his way through them.

'Sir?' Aurangzeb says, seeing the police. 'Shall we go back?'

'They will let us through,' The Lover says, dialling his cell phone with one hand. 'That's Inspector Sharma.'

'Let us through, Sharma. It is I. Yes, me. Arrest those two.'

There is a long pause on the other end of the line. The inspector takes a deep breath, his eyes on the Ganges.

'I will not do what the darkness says,' says the inspector.

'What rubbish are you speaking? Fool? Do you know who I …' The Lover realises that the inspector has hung up on him.

Open-mouthed, The Lover turns to Aurangzeb, not believing what has just happened. Then he emits a hysterical howl, mouth wide open, his scar pulsating. Aurangzeb freezes, stricken with fear, as The Lover screams some more.

The scream reaches Bencho and Iyer, who have just alighted from the roof, Iyer's staff in his hand.

'Sir,' Bencho says, his face going white as he notices the truck moving towards them in the distance, like a malevolent little beetle.

'Get back into your vehicle. Let them through,' the inspector barks at the constables.

'Bencho, get her back in,' Khanolkar shouts, and Bencho rushes to the front of the Tempo to capture Mala, who has escaped, her hair undone, waving an empty Bisleri bottle at a butterfly. She runs into the undergrowth and Bencho follows her, begging her to stop. Aurangzeb blows the horn as the truck picks up speed, sending cattle rushing off the road.

Iyer limps into the centre of the road, his coat flapping in the wind, his beard blowing over his shoulder, his staff in his hand.

Come.

Aurangzeb slows down upon seeing Iyer stride out, but The Lover jams the revolver into his side, and he touches the accelerator harder.

'Run over that dog. If you do not, I will kill you. I swear it,' The Lover tells Aurangzeb calmly.

Come. I am ready.

Licking his lips, his hands shaking, Aurangzeb accelerates, heading straight towards Iyer.

'Faster, bastard,' says The Lover, staring at Iyer, who stands like a statue, his staff held over his shoulder like a javelin, one leg stiff and dragging behind him.

'*Om Namashivaya Namaha,*' Iyer says. He is ready to die.

'Please,' screams Aurangzeb, now in tears, but The Lover is possessed. He wraps his arm around Aurangzeb's shoulders in an embrace, his eyes on Iyer, the little smile returning.

'Faster. Faster,' he whispers, his mouth foaming at the corners and his pupils dilated, the barrel jammed hard into Aurangzeb's ribs.

'Sir!' screams Bencho, who has just emerged from the forest, holding Mala. He rushes to desposit her in the Tempo.

Iyer hefts the staff and takes a deep breath.

I am Bhīma, tamer of elephants, master of the mace.

It is the right weight. It was always the right weight. He holds it in the middle, the staff balancing on the space between his thumb and forefinger.

We shall compose a poem, with songs, to explain these truths:
Even kings, if they break the law, have their necks wrung by dharma;
Great men everywhere commend Pattini of renowned fame;
And karma ever manifests itself, and is fulfilled.

Iyer feels that he knows the lance intimately, its length an extension of Iyer's own arm.

To wield a lance again.

Bencho pushes his way out of the Tempo and begins running towards Iyer with the despair of knowing he'll never reach him in time.

The truck's speedometer touches ninety as it hurtles towards Iyer.

Iyer sucks in his diaphragm and slows down his breathing, watching himself from elsewhere, willing the staff to become alive. He bends his knee and feels the meniscus move somewhat into place, as if it has a mind of its own.

Even though I knew it was a dream, I was powerless.

As the truck hurtles towards him, Iyer takes his arm back in one fluid movement, runs forward two steps with his eyes on The Lover, and launches the staff into the air. It sails through space, vibrating like a spear, and strikes the steering wheel, missing The Lover completely.

His legs apart, Iyer stands erect and places his hands on his hips, facing the truck speeding towards him. Aurangzeb tries to turn, but The Lover seizes the wheel and tries to align the truck with Iyer, who stands as still as a sculpture, staring him in the eye.

It is time.

A droplet of rain anoints his face.

The Lover turns the wheel but it does not turn. The staff has gone through it and hit the floor, preventing its rotation. The truck speeds towards the balustrade and the petrol tanker that has just driven onto the road.

Aurangzeb grabs at the wheel and attempts to swerve, but the truck is constrained to its path and misses the immobile Iyer by inches, his beard blowing sideways as it rushes past. It hits the balustrade and careens wildly, rising up on two wheels as The Lover yanks the staff out, too late. The truck crashes into the petrol tanker, which topples onto its side and is pushed sideways towards the bridge, both vehicles smashing through the barricade.

Policemen, drivers, cattle and barricades fly in all directions as the rain pours down. The rear doors of the truck swing open, the lock mutilated. The errand boy, accompanied by idols of various sizes and dimensions, falls out through the open doors and tumbles down the embankment towards the river. Unlike the idols, the skeletal errand boy, used to being thrown out of moving vehicles, lands on his feet in the shallows like a cat surrounded by broken gods, and hurries away, dodging the Nataraja that almost crushes him but lands in deeper water a few feet away. Miraculously, the vehicles do not catch fire, and skid to a rest, the driver's cabin of the truck mangled, an immense cloud of dust obscuring the truck. The petrol tanker's rear tap has broken off, sending petrol washing over the road and prompting its driver to jump out of the cabin and run away.

Pinned to his seat by the steering wheel, Aurangzeb is suspended upside down, his foot jammed in the mutilated chassis.

The Lover, shards of glass marking his face like tinsel, falls out of his seat, concussed. Choking on petrol fumes, he kicks his way out of the door window and crawls onto the road.

'Help me. I am stuck,' Aurangzeb begs, his leg trapped, the leather webbing of his sandal held by a steering rod. Ignoring him, The Lover crawls further away, regaining his senses and limping to the side of the road, where he stands for a few moments viewing the carnage before retreating into the shrubbery.

Aurangzeb can hear the inspector in the distance, shouting for everyone to abandon the truck, obscured from view by the cloud of dust its collision has caused.

'It will explode. Constables, make sure no one approaches the accident.' The inspector barks, using his *lathi* on a cowherd who is hovering nearby with a cell phone, videoing the accident.

'Help me,' Aurangzeb screams, struggling to free his foot. Petrol drips out of the broken tanker tap and into the cubicle, its pungent odour burning his nostrils.

Aurangzeb begins to beg in earnest, his eyes watering from the fumes, his clothes wet with petrol. He cries out for help, but the checkpoint has been abandoned except for a lone white cow a short distance away, chewing the cud disinterestedly.

'Help me. Please,' Aurangzeb shouts, just to hear his own voice. No one is there, he thinks; this is it. There is no sound apart from the river flowing under the bridge.

Aurangzeb thinks he hears coughing. Iyer chokes on the dust as he sloshes through puddles of rain towards the overturned truck.

'I have to stop him,' Bencho says, but the inspector orders him to be restrained.

'It will explode,' he says. 'You'll achieve nothing but killing yourself and saving no one.' He pushes Bencho towards the crowd that has receded some hundred yards down the road, Mala wailing with her head in her hands, and Damayanti trying with great effort to prevent her from running towards the accident.

'Hold them back. No one approaches the truck. Use your *lathis* if anyone tries,' the inspector shouts. The constables fan out across the road, *lathis* at the ready. He radios the checkpoint at the other end of the bridge, and they, too, block its access.

The dust is thick, but Iyer covers his nose and mouth with his lapels and follows Aurangzeb's cries. The throbbing in his head has increased, and Iyer leans against the truck, nausea rising in his gut. His knee is less stiff but still hurts terribly. Fighting the urge to vomit, he limps his way towards the crushed cubicle, blinded by the dust and rain. Falling onto his belly, Iyer finds the air is cleaner nearer the ground, and breathes easier. Pushing away the debris near the truck window, Iyer peers into the cubicle, letting his eyes adjust to the darkness. Iyer can just about make out a bloody, suspended Aurangzeb through a tangle of wire and shredded upholstery.

'You,' sobs Aurangzeb in despair, seeing Iyer look up at him.

'Mongoose! You! Did you pay the boy his money and make amends?' Iyer asks. Aurangzeb stares at Iyer in amazement, beginning to cry, but also surprised to find himself laughing at the same time, not believing what he has just heard.

'What?'

'Tell me the truth, toad. Did you say sorry?' Iyer lectures, wedging himself into a better position.

'Sir. Please, sir,' Aurangzeb says. 'Help me, please.'

'Did you give it to him or not?' Iyer asks, crawling into the cubicle, bending a windscreen wiper out of the way and just about managing to fit, so that he is face to face with the upside-down Aurangzeb.

'No. I did not,' Aurangzeb says, tears streaming up his forehead.

Iyer moves upward like a worm, trying to figure out how Aurangzeb is trapped. There is complete silence except for the sound of Bencho fighting with the constables, insisting that they let him help.

Iyer attempts to rise up to the crushed foot, which is pinned between the seat and the steering block, one of whose rods has gone through the leather of the sandal. He pulls on the leg but Aurangzeb's ankle is broken, and he bellows in pain each time it's touched. Grabbing onto the leg, Iyer tries to free the foot from the leather but, try as he might, it does not come free.

'Stop crying like a baby and help me here,' Iyer says impatiently, crouching back down, his face a few inches from Aurangzeb's.

'You are mad,' Aurangzeb says between heaving sobs, gasping for breath. He adds 'sir' as an afterthought.

'Listen to me,' Iyer says calmly, 'Can you get your foot out of your sandal?'

'I think … I don't know, sir,' he says, crying.

Crawling back into the tangle, Iyer comes back to the sandal. He tries with all his strength to tear it off with his hands, but the leather is too tough.

'What leather is this?' Iyer asks, genuinely curious but not waiting for an answer. He jams his head into the wires and grabs hold of the strap with his teeth, and begins to chew.

'It's … what most … I don't know, sir.'

'Well, it tastes like dung,' Iyer says, chewing.

Aurangzeb sniffs at the air. He can smell something burning. He tenses.

'Don't worry, my friend, you will be reborn a cockroach for sure,' Iyer says, still chewing at the leather, the odour from Aurangzeb's feet making him nauseous.

'The true taste of cow,' Iyer says, spitting bits of leather out of his mouth as the strap gives way.

Aurangzeb is still jammed. Moving backwards, Iyer gets his feet out of the cubicle and takes Aurangzeb's hand, trying to pull him free, his one good leg scrabbling for a foothold on the petrol-slicked road.

'Free yourself,' Iyer gasps as he struggles to heave Aurangzeb out of the cubicle. But his arms, burning with pain, are not strong enough. He grabs him around the chest, his arms beneath Aurangzeb's shoulders, and the upside-down Aurangzeb grabs him beneath his shoulders. Wrapped thus around each other, the sound of each other's hearts in their ears, Iyer pulls with all his strength.

'Ya Allah,' says Aurangzeb, closing his eyes, embracing Iyer tighter as he pulls Aurangzeb with a cry of '*Om Namashivaya Namaha*', his arms screaming for relief.

Groaning, Aurangzeb slithers from the tangle and out of the driver's seat. As Iyer continues to pull, a hand lands on Iyer's foot, pulling at him. He slides out of the truck, holding onto Aurangzeb, and they burst from the crushed cubicle onto the road. The hand is Bencho's; when Iyer looks at him he can see his clothes are torn and his face swollen from fighting with the constables.

They hobble away from the truck, Bencho helping Iyer, and Aurangzeb half hopping along. Flames crackle over the vehicle and into the cabin as it bursts into flames. They hobble on further as the truck really catches fire, the petrol combusting into flames rising twenty feet into the air, singeing the hair on their arms. They try to move faster, falling towards the bridge, the blaze hot on their backs, the air whipped into a fierce wind by the flames sucking oxygen into itself.

Aurangzeb falls and Iyer stumbles back towards him, half dragging him away from the inferno that now roars like a living thing. Bencho chokes and moves away, blinded by the white heat. A safer distance off, Iyer tries to lift up the dazed Aurangzeb, his arms beneath his knees and neck, but he is too heavy, and Iyer flops down onto the road, Aurangzeb cradled in his arms. Together, they catch their breaths, lit with the flames and buffeted by the wind and smoke.

'Sir,' whispers Aurangzeb.

'Yes,' croaks Iyer.

'Sorry. And thank you.'

'Shut up, baboon,' Iyer says, raising his head to the rain.

Iyer lowers him to the ground and gets shakily to his feet, the Tempo and everything else now obscured by the smoke.

It is done.

Iyer walks towards the railing and looks down at the water flowing beneath him, the bank strewn with idols and pieces of idols thrown from the truck when it toppled. The Durga on the tiger has landed upright in the shallows, the arm holding the sword emerging from the water. The errand boy and the Nataraja are nowhere to be seen. The white cow grazes by the roadside as if nothing has happened. A wind rises up from the river and blows the smoke away, and for a second, Iyer can make out the Inspector and Khanolkar holding back the instant crowd that has appeared from nowhere.

He sees Damayanti, vibrant blue and distant in the heated air, and Bencho, who walks towards Iyer, smiling widely.

'Sir!' cries Bencho in relief. The white cow wanders past, still chewing. The look on Bencho's face changes sharply when, to his utter disbelief, The Lover steps out of the undergrowth and pushes Iyer off the bridge.

35

Iyer lets his body go limp and falls like a stone.

I fly.

He hits the water hard, landing on his back. It stings, but it seems like someone else falls. Someone else has been hurt. The water closes over him. Another world. The back of his head feels as if someone has poured molten lead into it. His limbs go slack.

This too shall pass.

He sinks. Bubbles. Are they from his nose? The current turns Iyer. The horizon tilts from the shimmering surface. He sees Nataraja, the Lord of the Dance, completely immersed and poised upright on the riverbed, his dreadlocks alive.

Time is a circle.

Iyer sinks further, the surface darkened by smoke, lit by the flames. A shoal of tiny fish disperse and regroup, flashing like topaz. He feels the silt touch his back.

For a few seconds Iyer lies in the garden of wounded gods, limbs and torsos strewn around him like in the aftermath of a battle, the dreaming Vishnu lying on its side a short distance away.

The river is beginning to take away his breath. Soon it'll be over, he thinks, but with his arm working as if of its own accord, Iyer grasps the big toe on the left foot of the Lord of the Dance. The shoal of silver fish surrounds the god's countenance, ignoring the dying mortal at its foot. Then the minnows turn, catching the light, and the Lord of the Dance flicks his foot upwards, pushing Iyer towards the flames.

He rises as the petrol tanker explodes, turning the world white, then orange, blinding Iyer as he hovers mid river, engulfing The Lover and blowing him off the bridge.

As he loses consciousness he sees a crow flying in the smoke-stained sky through the tumultuous surface above. It circles and caws.

There you are.

Another form dives into the maelstrom, a blue goddess, her polyester-cotton sari shimmering around her as she swims towards Iyer, powerful arms and legs pushing back the water. She swims over the gods, scattering the silver fish, and reaches him. She grabs him under his arms, her blue garment unhitched and billowing around them like a celestial cloud. Kicking off the riverbed, she rockets towards the fire. Damayanti bursts out from the burning river, an unconscious Iyer in her arms.

36

I dreamt of our childhood house again.
Before my eyes it crumbled away, and all that remained was soil.

I smelled the earth.

The house was built with Ganges sand.

The monstrosity has melted away.

The lance in my hand does not crumble.

It rings when I draw it through the air. I leave it on the earth.

Instead of the well of damp granite, a river flows under the house. When I put my ear to the ground, I can hear it murmur.

I have found the Saraswati.

May you come into your own, brother. May you become what you are, no longer this person of this name or that name but the true self that is the being of all beings, my self and your self one.

I will write my memoirs in my own name, as it has already been written and already been read.

Kindly refer to me as Lalgudi Iyer. This is compulsory.

Kind regards,
Lalgudi Iyer

37

Damayanti carries Iyer towards the bank, and Bencho rushes into the water, taking him from her.

'Sir! Sir, my dear sir!'

Bencho lays him down on the bank, turning his head to the side to get the water out of his lungs. He holds his ear to Iyer's chest, his heart beating like a bird in a cage. Bencho shakes him and presses down on his chest several times. After a sharp breath Iyer gasps, vomiting the Ganges onto the sand.

'Sir!' cries Bencho, sobbing.

'He needs a hospital, and quick,' says the inspector, looking down on them from the road.

Damayanti emerges from behind the shrubbery, her hair in order and her sari retied. Old Mr Kapadia is wheeling about as well, trying to pilfer bits of shattered idols. The constables are given various orders and scurry about, photographing the idols with their phones and taking fragments of statues off the road. The constables are also having a tough time with the light-fingered crowd, now supplemented with passers-by, chasing a man with Lord Ganesha's head and wrestling with another to retrieve the hand of Shiva.

Aurangzeb is arrested and promises cooperation, thanking Iyer for saving his life before being led away.

'I think that it is a good idea that I keep him with us, just in case our big-shot friend sends someone else,' the inspector tells Bencho and Khanolkar.

The errand boy appears and helps Iyer into the inspector's jeep, whose canvas top has been charred. He cups Iyer's face as if he is a child, the same way Iyer had cupped his when he had beaten Aurangzeb.

Iyer is wrapped in blankets from the Tempo. The jeep doors are closed, the constables rip off the remnants of the charred canvas that hang in tatters, and they leave for Kashi. The inspector drives slowly so that the Tempo can keep up. Khanolkar is at the wheel, and the inmates of the home are mostly asleep, exhausted with all the excitement.

Iyer does not respond to conversation, feeling like a kite in the wind, the jeep's suspension not helping.

'I told you we would meet again,' chuckles the inspector. 'You have done the right thing today. I recommend you do not speak to the press, and I will make sure no hardship befalls you. OK?'

Iyer remains silent.

'Who would have thought that a lunatic like you would rescue the gods themselves!' jokes the inspector.

Footage of Iyer rescuing Aurangzeb, embracing each other upside down, faces in each other's chests, was shot on the cell phone of one of the watching crowd and uploaded to YouTube, and has already made it to the regional news. Iyer dozes through most of the journey. Mishra, informed by Khanolkar of their arrival, has already made an announcement to the local police and media that Lalgudi Krishnan Iyer, a patient of the home for the dying, has helped stop an international ring of antique smugglers, and also that Mr Khanolkar has helped the authorities in their operation.

Shortly thereafter, in another news segment, Jayachandra makes a statement condemning the illegal antiquities' trade, and praises the heroism of the senior citizen Iyer, more of the likes of whom the country needs, to overcome its challenges with corruption and intolerance.

Over the next day Iyer rests, hardly leaving his room as the visitors come by, including the police, who get Iyer to sign various statements, which he does without reading them.

The days pass, and despite the antibiotic course prescribed by the very worried Krishna, Iyer deteriorates, losing weight and developing a fever.

The rains begin in earnest and the Ganges goes into spate. Dr Krishna visits daily, hurrying through the rain and into Iyer's room. After his examinations, when he walks to the window, as is his custom, the young doctor sees debris floating down the river at high speed, coursing past the little boats held in place by snapping ropes.

On one such visit, while Krishna massages Iyer's legs the electricity fails, plunging the room into darkness.

'How are you feeling, Bhīma?' Krishna asks, and Iyer looks at a point a few inches behind Krishna's head.

'My name is Iyer.'

Khanolkar sends for a priest to come and visit Iyer. He attends Iyer early in the morning, before temple hours.

'He is all right. Just tired,' says the priest, and Khanolkar counts out his payment, note by note, without angst.

Damayanti and Bencho come by that evening, Bencho dressed in his best shirt, hair combed. Damayanti's eyes are puffy from crying. She brings a small dish wrapped in a cloth. They visit Khanolkar.

'How is he?'

'The doctors say he is fine, but I am not sure. Maybe he is ready,' replies Khanolkar, entering the latest Iyer-related expense into his ledger without increasing it. 'Why do you look so sad? He has led a full life,' says Khanolkar, snapping the ledger shut and opening another. 'Too full, maybe.'

'He has always been so kind to me. I wish that Panchakanya would come now to see him. They say love works miracles. I hope she comes. What ungratefulness to ignore him now!' Damayanti says, furious that the love of Iyer's life has abandoned him in his hour of need.

'I don't think that Panchakanya will come, Damayanti,' Khanolkar says, clasping his hands together and looking at Damayanti over his ledgers.

'Yes. These days' women ...' Damayanti sniffles.

'I have something to tell you, Damayanti.'

'Yes?'

'Please sit down.'

'No, I will stand.'

'Please sit down.'

'OK.'

And Khanolkar tells her.

38

'Don't be sad, sir,' Bencho says at Iyer's bedside. 'They say you have fallen silent. Get off that bed, let's go out wandering again. If you think your defeat by Bakasura is the cause of your depression, we can call for a rematch, and this time I know you will win. You yourself have told me that defeat is an essential part of victory. The defeated of today will become the victors of tomorrow? No?' Bencho asks, looking tenderly down at Iyer.

'We have been spared the utter desolation and horror of a life's success, Bencho. If I had killed Bakasura, I might cease to exist completely. What reason would there be to *be*, then? Besides, I have learned more about myself when my body struck the Ganges: all was illuminated.'

'Yes, sir? What was illuminated?'

Iyer does not reply and focuses on his breathing, going back to the place in between – in between the fire and the riverbed, suspended in the water, trying to find the right words to reveal what he'd seen.

'When you empty your head of thinking, your soul breaks its chains. Dormant selves rise, and you become what you are,'

Iyer says, the room swimming about him, the shoal of shiny fish flickering like the stars by the window.

'Sir, my dear sir, there can be only one you.'

'No Bencho, nothing is original. I am the combined entity of everyone I've been, in all my lives. I am no more original than the ghosts in my dreams.'

'Sir, what was illuminated when you struck the river?' asks Bencho, bringing Iyer back to what he had been about to reveal.

'You recall that I hit my head on a *shivalinga*, and was given knowledge of a previous birth, Bencho, not that long ago?'

'Yes, sir!'

'This time when I struck the water, watched over by the Nataraja, raised by his foot, I received *spiritual* knowledge of other lives, Bencho.'

'Sir! What were you? A warrior? A king? A sage in the upper reaches of the Himalayas? A yogi in the lower reaches of Mount Kailash? No, I know!' he says, excitedly. 'A tiger!'

'Where is that dream diary of mine? I have so much to write down. Quick, before these thoughts pass.'

'Sir, who will write our story?' Bencho asks, looking for Iyer's notebook, his eyes filling with tears.

'I do not know. But the author will have to lead a pure life himself to allow the truth of our story to flow through him. Or you, Bencho. Or maybe I will write it. Maybe in this life. Or maybe in another.'

Bencho hums,

> *May the goddess of speech enable us to attain all*
> *possible eloquence,*
> *She who wears on her locks a young moon,*
> *Who shines with exquisite lustre, who sits reclined on a*
> *white lotus,*

And from the crimson cusp of whose hands pours,
radiance on the implements of writing,
And books produced by her favour.

'We are nothing, Bencho. We are the poems that will be forgotten. But they will reappear in other ages like those river dolphins we saw.'

'Sir?'

Iyer mutters something, but Bencho does not hear what he says.

'Sir?' asks Bencho again, but Iyer has fallen asleep.

Bencho waits for a while, then retreats from the room and walks down the stairs, passing Mishra, who stands by a motionless Khanolkar, who's leaning against the wall as if he has been waiting for Bencho. They acknowledge each other, making eye contact and nodding, Bencho standing straight as they pass each other in the spiral, equals for the first time.

Iyer sleeps, and Panchakanya appears to him dressed like a mythological queen from the *Mahabharata* TV serial.

'My dear sir! Do not leave me,' she entreats, bedecked with costume jewellery and gold.

'I am grateful that you come to me in my last hours. I have always been true to you, Panchakanya,' Iyer says, half waking into a fever.

'I am Damayanti, and I am flesh and blood. My name is not Panchakanya. I do not want you to die,' says the queen, her ethereal sari turning into a white polyester-cotton blend, her luminous body turning into Damayanti, who has entered the room with a dish and some bandages in her hands, awakening Iyer.

'Damayanti?' Iyer says, opening his eyes and turning his head to her, his breath slowing, 'Such a significant name.'

'You must be hungry.'

Damayanti unwraps the dish from its cloth and puts it down by his bed.

'And I am Iyer, Lalgudi Iyer,' he says, trying to sit up on his bed.

'What happened to Bhīma?'

'Bhīma is still around.'

'And Bakasura? And all the other monsters?'

'They are still about,' Iyer says, wincing with the effort of trying to sit up. He gives up and lies flat on his back again.

'Lalgudi Iyer,' she says, looking down at his body, the wounds and scars of his quest marking his skin like a map. 'You need to rest. Now sit up and unbutton your shirt,' she orders. For the first time in many years, Iyer listens and obeys.

'You will not leave this room until you are better,' Damayanti says, even more sternly.

'All this has happened before,' mumbles Iyer, abruptly reaching out and touching the acid scars on Damayanti's face. She freezes but then makes herself relax, and lets Iyer use his finger to trace the outline of the burn. He closes his eyes and watches his own breath as he does, like a wind in a desert, deep and even. Iyer opens his eyes and she is still there, unchanged, and it is like seeing her for the first time. Iyer's heart swells and he is overwhelmed with joy.

'Damayanti,' he says, his eyes closing again, the sound of her name clear to him for the first time. 'Damayanti.'

'So many wounds? How did you get so many?' she notices a weeping cut on his chest, changing the subject and picking up a washcloth from a bowl of diluted Dettol.

'I followed my intuition,' Iyer says, chuckling.

'Tell me. Tell me,' Damayanti says, as though talking to a child, soaking the washcloth and squeezing out the excess Dettol into the bowl.

'This is from my fight to free the prisoners, dedicated to you of course,' he says, pointing at the scar on his forehead. 'They opened my third eye,' he says, laughing. 'Here is my scar from my battle with that driver Aurangzeb.' He points to the healing splinter wound between his fingers.

'They are not fully healed,' Damayanti says, wiping his forehead.

'That's because they are from this life,' replies Iyer, 'but they will find their healing, somewhere, someday, in some life or the other. Or their revenge.'

'What other lives?'

Iyer closes his eyes and goes back to the river, the Ananta uncoiling, Vishnu still dreaming, Kaliyug alive, the flames above him and the broken gods below. He runs his hands over his body, searching out the blows from different times. His hands stop at his face – the left side – and he tells her what has consumed him since falling from the bridge.

'You know that driver Aurangzeb? The man I beat up.'

'Yes, everybody knows how you beat up poor Aurangzeb.'

'I was other lives besides Bhīma.'

'Ah, aren't we all?' Damayanti says sweetly, dabbing at a wound with the rag.

'I was another Aurangzeb once upon a time, the Alamgir himself, the defeater of a war elephant, the scourge of Hindus and the sixth Mughal emperor,' Iyer says slowly, pointing at a barely visible birthmark on his forehead above the star-shaped wound.

'What great battle wound was this?'

'Not a wound. I slipped as I was about to do my *namaz* and hit my forehead on the floor.'

'You were a Muslim in another life?'

'Yes. You were there too.'

'Who was I to you, then, in that life?' Damayanti asks, running the cool cloth over his hot skin.

'You were my brother Dara,' Iyer says laughing.

'Why are you laughing?'

'My other brother, Murad, is known as Mr Khanolkar today. And in that life I imprisoned both of you,' Iyer stops laughing and looks at her.

'Is that so?' Damayanti says. 'Your body is a vessel of past lives?'

'Yes. I think so.'

'And from which life did this come?' she asks, pointing to a discoloured patch of skin near his temple.

'That is a sword wound and ...' Iyer finds he can't continue; tears roll down his cheeks.

'Why are you crying?'

'Because I know who gave me that wound.'

'Who did? Bencho?'

'No. You did. And you also had me hanged.'

'What? I do not understand ...'

'You went by the name Brigadier General Neill and the year was 1857, at Kanpur, my dear.'

'My God, I was a Britisher? Why did I kill you, a respectable Brahmin, like that?'

'I was not a Brahmin then, though you killed many Brahmins too.'

'If you were not a Brahmin, what were you?'

'I was a man named Gungoo Mehter and I killed many people that day.'

'How cruel the British were, to do that. And stop talking about such horrifying things, Bhīma,' Damayanti says, wiping his lips with a rag.

'I was executed for a terrible crime, Damayanti. And they responded with even greater ones.'

Damayanti looks hard at his face. 'I am not the killing kind, Iyer. And neither are you,' she says, now a little exasperated at the tone of the conversation.

'We are as we are, we will be what we were not and we shall become what we hate,' Iyer says, and lets his hands travel again, moving down over his throat and into the plains ahead, over his chest and down his left arm to the hand, where his fingers twitch. Iyer begins to laugh, and though no sound of laughter is heard, tears trickle down his face.

'Yes?' asks Damayanti. 'What did I do to you now?'

'Here is where I lost my hand at the battle of Lepanto, fighting the Ottomans, in 1571, defending that group of villages we now call Europe,' Iyer says, pointing at a mole on his left wrist. 'I was a Spaniard then.'

'That's not a big wound,' Damayanti says sceptically.

'It was Bencho who fired that cannon shot that blew off my hand.'

'Bencho! Ha! Finally someone else. Who was Bencho? Tell me.'

'He was a slave named Hameed owned by the Ottomans, descended from Tenali Ram, formerly a warrior in the employ of the Vijayanagara king, Rama Raya, captured at the battle of Talikota and sold to some Turkmenistanis as a gunner who was to serve under the Turks in the battle at Lepanto. Bencho – I mean Hameed – lit the wick of the cannon that blew off my hand. I was captured and made a galley slave, and I ended up sharing a bench with him, as he had been demoted for bad accuracy, thievery and poetry. I nicknamed him Bhantaki, or what he called a *brinjal* in his language. Black as a *brinjal*, that drunken Bencho was. Hameed Bhantaki,' Iyer chuckles.

'So you knew Bencho before. And me, too?'

'You were my maid Aldonza in Spain then.'

'Ah, was she beautiful?'

'No. She was an ugly woman who made extra money by whoring on the side, and she hated me very much.'

'Why? For calling her such terrible things? Definitely.'

'No, my dear, for not paying you your total fee.'

Damayanti opens her mouth in shock and then bursts out laughing, covering her mouth with her hand.

'What a story!' she laughs. 'You really know how to spin a tale.'

Iyer looks confused and then smiles.

'That Hameed Bhantaki had such wonderful stories to tell me. So much time chained and rowing, chained and rowing, rowing and chained. I think when you're chained the spirit is set free and when you're freed, the spirit chains itself. If it wasn't for that scoundrel Hameed, I might not have made it. That *brinjal* was a gift from heaven.'

Damayanti feels his forehead and it burns. 'Your fever is rising.'

'How we laughed, Damayanti. In the midst of such pain, we laughed.'

'You have known Bencho a long time, Iyer!'

'A somewhat useless fellow for the most part, but nonetheless a poet floating through the ages. A bumbling lump of loyal corruption,' he says, laughing.

'Poet through the ages?'

'Yes, he was so many. Asvaghosha, Kalidasa, Bharavi, and then later, when Kaliyug struck, Hameed and that fellow who sounds like a saucer.'

'OK, Iyer, that's enough. At least I know who we are now.'

'All our lives yesterday are also our lives today. I have lost count, as we were beasts and plants too, my dear, but the wonderings of ants, the musings of banana plants and the philosophies of crocodiles might not make for proper conversation today. Our atoms have been there from first light, from first sound,' Iyer says, fatigue coming over him.

'You knew me in all lives? In all those different worlds?'

'*Om Namah Shivaya*. We have been together from the beginning,' he says, taking a deep breath. 'And this too shall pass.'

'And what of Bakasura and your quest for the immortal, which the whole ghat is chatting about now?'

Iyer pauses, his eyes closed, thinking hard and then relaxing.

'When I felt I should slay evil demons, I have brought my own self close to death; when I thought I had journeyed deep into the darkness of this age, I have come to the centre of my own; and where I thought I would find a slavering demon, I discovered the Nataraja himself.'

'And now? Will you run away again?'

'When I had thought myself to be alone, I have been with you, since the beginning.'

'What about us?' Damayanti asks, softly, unsure of what Iyer is saying but overcome with a sudden feeling of tenderness. Iyer remains silent as she squeezes out the rag and spreads it over his forehead, looking down at his cartography marked with keloids for hills, cuts for valleys and bruises for earth, no fat obscuring the details.

'Most waste life living in the future and the past.'

'What about us?'

'I am here with you, now.'

'Do not die, Iyer,' she says, her voice breaking. 'And why did you not share all this with me earlier? Why not tell everyone who you've shared lives with?'

'It is like I am on a boat in the river. I sail downstream and you row upstream. We pass close – so close that if I reach out I could touch you – but during the journey, the waters are rough and the oars need managing. When our boats pass, we are too busy rowing to even look. And life passes.'

Damayanti can feel her heart contracting; she can't speak, and takes a few breaths to steady herself.

'Tomorrow I will visit Kashi Vishwanath temple and offer up prayers for you,' she says with forced brightness.

'Tomorrow I will leave to battle. The demon awaits!'

'You are not going anywhere. You will relearn how to live,' Damayanti says, and a wind rushes into the window, bringing with it some orange blossoms from the Gulmohar tree.

Spring.

Iyer closes his eyes. The tiredness returns. He feels like the world is whirling around him, but is comforted by Damayanti's words.

A brass band is passing by: another funeral procession. Rose-ringed parakeets fly overhead like shrieking green comets. Iyer sees them from behind his eyelids.

'Iyer,' she whispers, trying to wake him, but Iyer is in a place beyond words.

Damayanti sees a contusion has spread out over his sternum like a rose, where Krishna had pressed down on him with his staff. An infection seems to have set into its scratches, and it radiates outward from his heart – tributaries from a spring-fed lake, rays from a child's sun – meeting the blue veins in his shoulders, rising to his throat and flowing into his arms. She caresses its progress, following the dark veins as if they are tributaries. She touches his lips with her fingers and feels his breath on her fingertips.

He breathes.

She places her face over his and closes her eyes. She feels his exhalation on her forehead, the hum of his breath on her burns. She hears his heart, her ear over the star, and the sound of it passes through her, filling the room, flowing out of the window, rushing down the streets and becoming the water that flows over the land. Her tears fall on him.

Wiping her eyes dry, Damayanti bends over the map of his adventures – in this life and the others – and, closing her eyes, she kisses his heart.

39

This time he would have to plan ahead, dreams Iyer.

While the dying slept, he would pack a bag with some clothes and basic weaponry. He would rise early and conceal the bag under his jacket. Then he would insist on walking down to the mess for breakfast, being helped down the stairs, making a show of it, exclaiming in pain perhaps. He would eat well and request to sit in the little sunlight to warm his aching knees. Given his pitiful state, Khanolkar would never suspect an abscondence, and permission would be granted. On the way to the platform by the river, which he would hobble towards, pausing from time to time in case anyone was watching, Iyer would remove a bamboo staff from the funeral stretcher that awaited him in the courtyard.

Once on the stone platform and left to his own devices, he would stand on his good leg and use the bamboo as a crutch to limp down to the balconies where the beggars thronged.

Bencho would help, of course, but not so early in the adventure, as Bencho was likely to insist that Iyer regain his strength before running off again. So Bencho would not be informed. The surly leper, on the other hand, would be essential. Iyer would strike a deal with him for protection and transport. He would haggle for a place on the pushcart in exchange for riches and fame beyond the craven leper's wildest dreams. The leper would be a hard negotiator, no doubt – given the degenerate criminal he surely was – but Iyer, as always, would prevail, using wisdom and divine bribery to get his way.

The leper had mentioned something about Bombay, and the idea of a new city appealed to Iyer. They would leave for Bombay, the leper pushing the cart, the promise of fame and riches filling his crumbling body with strength and his surviving fingers with endurance. They would head west towards Allahabad and then onto Kanpur, and Khanolkar would not suspect a thing as they fled, scouring the banks of the river as they made good their escape via land. They would beg for food from travellers and sleep under the night sky, as few attacked lepers except for other lepers, but Iyer would arm himself with the staff in any case. They would work their way southwest from there, onward to Indore – that dividing city between the Deccan and Delhi, built as protection from both the Marathas and Mughals – where they would rest for a few weeks before walking to Bombay, formerly a mangrove swamp – an ideal habitat for demons.

There would be a good chance that he would contract leprosy, but the affliction would be advantageous to his quest, as lepers are seldom searched or suspected. And if he looked pathetic enough, it could be a valuable disguise. It was also likely that suffering in this life for the right reasons would assist Iyer in his next incarnation, where he could be reborn into a better avatar, a bottlenosed dolphin perhaps. Or if he were lucky, he'd be reborn a whale – once closely related to man, but who had chosen to remain in the ocean and develop inward over millennia, perfecting senses, communication, love and awareness unlike man, who had chosen the other direction.

Afflicted with the gift of leprosy, a gift because no home would take him, Iyer would hunt down Bakasura and his minions, who'd be unprepared for the apocalypse that awaited them. He would, of course, have to be careful with the surly leper, as it was certain in Iyer's mind that he would try to kill, or at the very least, rob him once they were out of the city. He would have to be alert. But the leper only had two fingers, and however strong they may be, Iyer was an incarnation of Bhīma.

Fingerless palms would not allow him the skillful use of the mace, and with missing limbs he might not survive a horde of demons taking different forms. One of his knees is useless, but there is still strength left in the other one: Iyer kicks off the sheet to test it. His head throbs with fever but Iyer smiles to himself, stretching out on the bed like a cat, savoring the excitement of making plans.

ACKNOWLEDGEMENTS

Many people inspired this book, consciously and unwittingly. In particular I am deeply grateful to:

Irina Snissar for her love, criticism and forbearance while I wrote this story.

My parents Dr. Aloma and David Lobo for their example, faith, love and goodness, without which so much might have been so different.

My sister Nisha for her patience and wisdom.

Dr Ashok Krishnan for his kind encouragement, mentorship, friendship and guidance, both literary and otherwise.

Faiza S. Khan, my editor at Bloomsbury, for having faith in this story and for her incredible role in the formation of this book.

Mr Suchindranath Aiyer for sharing his story, thoughts and historical views.

Mr K.V.K. Murthy for his writing, example and integrity.

Vikramajit Ram for his listening ear and kind advice.

Eric Strauss, Shantulan Mishra and Adarsh N.C. for their companionship and support during so many adventures on the Ganges and elsewhere.

The 'Knights of the Square Table', the universe at the end of Koshy's Restaurant, Prem Koshy for his generosity, spirit of adventure, expertise regarding aliens and talent to create minor cataclysms of the storytelling sort.

Nausheer Hameed for his cheerfulness, humour and wit, no matter the cataclysm.

Darius 'Tuffy' Taraporvala for his calm and conversation.

D.P. Sridhar for his measured silence, style and integrity in all circumstances.

Ravi Khanolkar for his gentle rage against the machine.

Dr N.V.S. Krishnan for his wisdom, stories and deep suspicion of all things worthy of deep suspicion.

Reverend Peter Anirudh for setting the example of how to be a good man in dark times.